THE BEAR

IN THE MIDDLE OF BETWEEN

A NOVEL BY ALEXIS ACKER-HALBUR

Kirk House Publishers

ISBN: 978-1-933794-99-0

Library of Congress Number: Pending

For permission requests, write to the publisher at the address below:

Kirk House Publishers
1250 East 115th Street
Burnsville, MN 55337
KirkHousePublishers.com

Ordering Information:
Quantity sales. Special discounts are available on quantity purchases by corporations, associations, and others. For details, contact the publisher at the address above.

Printed in the United States of America

IN THE MIDDLE OF BETWEEN

In the middle of between there is no room
for indecision; only room enough
to be alone, in the middle of the road.
I can see the light at both ends, but which
end do I travel, which way is the correct end.
In the middle of between.

From one end to the other, to and fro and back
again at the midpoint, where do I stand on
any given point in the midst of knowing
too little, unable to reach the peak.
Never empty, never full, there is no mean –
In the middle of between.

—Alexis Acker-Halbur

ACKNOWLEDGEMENT

There is no greater gift than to acknowledge the people who have made my life and writing so blessed. This was a difficult story to write, but I am constantly surrounded by people who see and support my life's mission.

To my wife and soulmate, Rita Acker-Halbur; my editors, Gerry Sasse and Connie Anderson; my publisher, Ann Aubitz; my Women of Words (WOW) East beta readers and members; and of course, the Divine Spirit.

You make me believe.

AAH

TABLE OF CONTENTS

CHAPTER ONE |9

CHAPTER TWO |12

CHAPTER THREE |23

CHAPTER FOUR |30

CHAPTER FIVE |33

CHAPTER SIX |52

CHAPTER SEVEN |57

CHAPTER EIGHT |67

CHAPTER NINE |71

CHAPTER TEN |74

CHAPTER ELEVEN |88

CHAPTER TWELVE |94

CHAPTER THIRTEEN |112

CHAPTER FOURTEEN |118

CHAPTER FIFTEEN |125

CHAPTER SIXTEEN |143

CHAPTER SEVENTEEN |164

CHAPTER EIGHTEEN |170

CHAPTER NINETEEN |181

CHAPTER TWENTY |184

CHAPTER TWENTY-ONE |190
EPILOGUE |199
ABOUT THE AUTHOR |200
RESOURCES |201

CHAPTER ONE

There is no chance, no destiny, no fate, that can hinder the firm resolve of a determined soul.
—Unknown

My car's wiper blades could not control the cascade of ice and snow falling on the windshield. The wiper's rapid attempts to clear the window synced in rhythm with my thoughts. I have no hope, no escape, no relief. My tires slip and slide through the blizzard like a drunk swaying out of a bar.

The drifting and brutal winds sent white waves of snow across the four-lane highway. I needed to be cautious and watchful. This is no weather to end up in the ditch.

Determination was my co-pilot, occupying the rider's seat, nudging me onward. I had left extra early, before there was any chance the state patrol would close the highway.

Woman against winter, I was in an extreme laugh/cry mood. Part of my mind kept wandering into the recesses of my memory. Two words kept popping up: *Why me?*

I glanced down at my white knuckles clutching the steering wheel. Returning my gaze to the road, I had one more exit until, by luck and determined insanity, I spotted my exit. I knew the campground was the third right turn on County Road 23. The welcome sign to Banning State Park was not visible in the storm, but I knew by instinct where and when to turn. There was the entrance sign, stating "Closed for Camping."

When I arrived at the park office, I thanked my car for delivering me to my destination unscathed. The sign in the window said, "No camping."

"No shit, Sherlock," I said out loud to the sign. Here it is the middle of February, and a blizzard is in full force. No sane person would venture out to a closed state park in a winter storm except for a fool like me.

◆◆◆◆◆

After a short and frigid hike, I arrived at the 14-foot cliff overlooking the Kettle River. I adjusted my backpack on my hips and clutched my walking stick. I came to Banning in the middle of a cold and snowy blizzard with one purpose: *escape my demons by ending my life.*

The barrenness of the park matched the emptiness inside me.

Removing my backpack and placing it on the snow, I withdrew the gun I had purchased last week. The cold from the gray metal seeped through my mittens.

I could hear water rushing along the open rapids about a half-mile down from where I stood. A sudden realization occurred to me. It would be late spring before anyone discovered my body, that is, if someone actually found me. Being trapped at the bottom of the rapids could keep my body down for several months. If I fell backward and landed on the cold, heartless river's ice and rocks, my spine would break into fragments, and my neck would snap as the bullet pierced my brain.

After struggling to remove my mittens, I finally placed the gun in my mouth. I aimed the barrel toward my brain when a sudden swirling cyclone of snow came barreling at me. A big black object in the snow's center rushed toward me like a tsunami as I tried to yank the gun out of my mouth.

My lips let go as I was pummeled backward by the force. I heard the blast and felt red hot fire on my forehead. I fought for solid ground under my boots, but I was falling over the cliff. I could feel myself in the air along with the black blur.

Then there was only silence—dead silence.

CHAPTER TWO

The woods are lovely, dark, and deep.
But I have promises to keep,
and miles to go before I sleep,
and miles to go before I sleep.
— Robert Frost

The smell was horrible and unrelenting. I cracked open my eyes to see what was causing the stink. My mind took a moment to adjust to the sight. A large black bear was staring at me, its sharp teeth bared.

I shut my eyes as fear paralyzed my limbs. How could I be lying on the ground with a black bear hovering over me? What happened? Where was I? The ache in my head was throbbing and the smell was repugnant. I felt an icy breeze on the side of my head.

Everything I have read on bear attacks indicated that black bears do not attack humans. The park brochure I read that summer had warned me if a bear did attack me, I needed to refrain from moving and pretend I was dead. I shut my eyes against the sight and stink.

"Grrrrr," the bear growled as its dripping saliva hit my face. It stunk even more than the bear's breath. "Grrrrr," it roared again. I felt the bear slide away from me.

Opening my eyes, I noticed the bear retreating to the back of a living room-sized cave. Some light made it through the opening of the cave, giving me a chance to gather my senses. I lay very still.

As my mind cleared, I remembered my suicide attempt on the overlook. Realizing the blur in the snow was this black bear, I remembered falling off the cliff. Wait! A black bear attacked me even though I know bear attacks are rare. "I must be special."

Was I dead? No, I was alive and about to be dinner for this bear. I looked at the bear in the distance. It had not moved closer and, in fact, seemed to stay away from me. The bear let out a low-volume string of grunts as she paced back and forth. I tried to sit up, but my muscles shook beyond my control. My head ached as I realized with shock that I could not move. My neck was the source of tremendous pain, and I took several deep breaths hoping that it would help. Fifteen minutes passed before I could coordinate my legs and arms. I propped myself onto my side and then into a sitting position. The bear growled, but the sound was not one of fright or anger. I looked at the bear and saw something sticking out of its fur.

"My walking stick," I said aloud to the bear. I tried to shake my head, but fire raced through my neck and body. I reached up and felt my forehead. Fresh blood covered a gash on the left side of my head above my eyebrow. I winced, trying to gauge the severity of the wound.

"Is this the afterlife?" I asked the bear. It looked at me like I was an annoyance.

I was in shock. How else could I be in this situation, sitting in a cold cave with an injured bear? Either that or I was dead, although would I be able to feel pain or even think if I were dead?

"Grrrrrr," I heard the bear grunt. The bear, too, was in a lot of pain because of the embedded stick in its shoulder hump.

I tried to stand without moving my head. The pain was unbelievable followed by wave after wave of nausea. Attempting to stand on my feet, I grabbed the wall of the cave. The cave spun around for what seemed like an eternity. The next thing I knew I vomited.

"Do people puke when they're dead?" I thought after catching my breath. My breath reeked as bad as the bear's. I glanced at the bear in sympathy. My legs shook as my hands felt the cold wall. Like the bear, I was also in pain.

Why was the bear not hibernating? That was my last question before I crumpled to the frozen ground.

◆◆◆◆◆

A low sound vibrated my body and made my head and neck hurt more. I opened my eyes again, wondering where I was and how I got there. The sound was so full of pain that my heart responded with sadness and a feeling of deep despair. The black bear was moaning.

I knew the bear with the white patch of fur on her chest was a female because her neck and ears were smaller than a male bear. She was hurting, but I had no idea how to help the injured bear. Of course, I did not believe I had the strength to remove the walking stick. I so wanted the sound to stop because that painful, lonely sound made my soul weep.

I knew helping an injured bear would be suicide, but what difference did it make when I was already dead.

Gathering what little strength I could muster, I inched my way up with the help of the cave wall. I shuffled toward the back of the cave. The bear was down on its knees with its large paws madly trying to reach the stick in its shoulder.

"Grrrrrr," the roar became a whimper.

I decided if, indeed, I was dead I had no reason not to try. The thought gave me a sense of surreal confidence. Painstakingly, I got on my knees and looked toward the bear.

"Um, Ms. Bear, I'd like to help you," my voice shook as did my hands. I took off my mittens and saw blood covering my left hand. "I'm going to pull that stick out of your fur, but I know it's going to hurt you," I whispered managing to stand on shaking legs and struggling to get to the cave's opening. In the light, I saw what looked like drag marks on the ground. I realized then that the injured bear must have dragged me from the river and into the cave. But why? With effort, I broke off an icicle hanging from the opening of the cave.

"I'm an idiot!" I conceded to myself as I neared. "But I'm dead so why not."

When I was three feet away from the bear, I held out the large icicle in my naked right hand. The bear blinked and opened its mouth showing its teeth.

"I want to help you," I implored again, feeling the chill from the ice. The bear did not move.

Finding the strength, I staggered closer to her. "Shhh, you're going to be fine." I laid the icicle on her fur next to the stick. The bear's growl was more of a plea than a warning. I left the icicle there for several minutes. When I removed it, I felt her fur. It was very cold, and I hoped it had numbed the area around the stick. I tossed the icicle down on the dirt floor.

Without a second thought I pulled at the stick.

"Roarrrrrrrrrrrr!" A large paw swung out and hit me in my stomach. I bent over and fell back from the impact. My whole body screamed.

"Shit!" I cried out. Blood trickled down my forehead and lips.

The stick was still embedded. I knew that the decorative nubs I left on the stick were now a disadvantage for the bear. I gasped several deep breaths trying to calm my nerves. I wiped my bloody hands on my pants.

Once I caught my breath, I retrieved the icicle from the dirt and placed it on the bear's fur. For the second time today, I felt determined insanity, this time to help the injured bear. Moments seemed like hours.

Again, I threw down the icicle and grabbed the stick with both hands and pulled. As the bear moved in the opposite direction from me, the stick slid out with such force, I flew across the cave. When I landed hard on the ground, I shook my head. The blood spurted from the gash on my forehead and dripped into my eye. I grew nauseated again and withdrew a mitten from my jacket pocket. I covered the gash with it. I could feel the sticky blood seep through the material, all the while the bear grunted and growled.

The smell of blood was revolting.

I passed out.

◆◆◆◆◆

"Thank you, Claudia Matthews."

The deep voice pierced through the pain in my head and neck as I struggled to regain consciousness. A pile of dried leaves buffered my head as I lay on my back.

"What?" I struggled to get up, but the pain in my neck made me dizzy.

"Lay down," the voice commanded, "you're hurt."

I opened my eyes to see the bear's face within inches of my own. My body began to shake violently. Standing, the bear was at least six feet tall and weighed about 300 pounds. I wondered why it was not in hibernation, or I woke it up in my attempt to end my life.

The bear moved behind me and crouched down, placing its paws over me. I felt the warmth of the fur and the big body. I knew I was dreaming because this bear was hugging me.

"Bear hugs," I said to myself and smiled.

I knew at that moment I was truly insane and very dead.

◆◆◆◆◆

I may not be sane, but I am still Claudia Matthews currently hovering between life and death. I want to escape the injustices Life threw at me, but I also do not want the finality that comes with Death. In this space, there is everything and there is nothing. There is both white and black, light and dark, silence and sound, and warm and cold. I do not feel love or pain. I simply exist.

When my eyes open, I am greeted with a new landscape. Unbelievably, I was not in a cave, but in campsite thirty-three. Daylight was emerging over the pine trees and I smelled the earthy tones of my surroundings. The air had a chill to it as I sat in front of a leaping fire wrapped in a soft wool blanket. The trees were budding so I guessed it was a spring day. The steaming cup of coffee, in an earthen mug, swirled its aromatic smell in and out of my nostrils. With a deep breath in and out, I did not want to hurry the pleasure.

"You're awake, Claudia," chatted a voice to my left.

I carefully turned my head as not to cause more pain and saw the same black bear, with the white tuft on its chest. Now the huge creature was sitting on its haunches and looking at me with big black eyes.

"Hey, how do you know my name?" I asked with wide eyes. "You're a talking bear?"

"Yes, in fact, I am," the bear spoke perfect English.

I groaned. Death was not what I had expected. I had never thought about what Death would be like, but a talking bear was more than my imagination could absorb.

My swollen lips came together in a smirk.

"Why are you smiling?"

"I'm not smiling, I'm smirking," came my reply. I was looking at this huge bear and wondering why I was not scared. "I'm smirking because I'm talking to a live bear who speaks perfect English."

The bear tilted her head as if examining me.

Finally, I said, "How do you know my name?"

"I know many things about you."

"Then who are you because bears don't talk to humans."

"You don't look surprised," the bear said.

"I'm not." I struggled to sit straighter and sipped more hot coffee from the mug. I relished the warm liquid going down my dry throat. "I'm dead or at least I'm somewhere between Life and Death. "

"Because talking bears only appear in animated movies."

"Something like that." I sipped more coffee. The hot liquid tasted so good I doubted that it was real.

"Tell me something," the bear asked.

"What?" I tried to shrug.

"Why did you try to kill yourself today?"

"Today?" my confusion at the word "today" bothered me. "You mean yesterday or a week ago?"

"No, I mean today," the bear said, "this afternoon during the snowstorm."

I looked around the campsite seeing no snow. "I…I'm…"

"I know you don't understand but you're hurt, and you need to rest."

"How did I get hurt?" My body screamed with pain every time I moved.

"We tumbled over the cliff together," the bear explained and added, "I was able to only redirect the bullet."

I raised my hand to my head, felt the gash with my fingers, and felt the matted blood in my short brown strands. "Guess you missed your chance at dinner."

"I'm a vegetarian," the bear stuck out its long red tongue. "You didn't answer my question. Why did you try to kill yourself?"

I peered down at my hands imagining the gun. Where was it? Most likely, it was at the bottom of the overlook buried in the snow and big rocks. I cringed, thinking about a young boy finding it this spring and shooting his hand off. I needed to retrieve it.

As if the bear could read my mind, I saw a shiny object on the ground near its right paw. It was the gun.

"What the…" I stammered.

"You don't need this anymore."

I blinked and the gun disappeared.

"For a third time, I'll ask why you tried to kill yourself." The six feet tall bear towered over me and the campfire.

"I had enough."

"Enough of what?"

"Everything…" It struck me that I was talking in English to a bear. "Hey, how come you can speak English?"

"You have a lot of questions."

"Yeah, I've never been dead before."

"To answer your question, I learned English as a cub. I also speak several languages: German, Spanish, Chinese, French, and Ojibwa. I prefer speaking bear most."

"Impressive," I replied. Closing my eyes, I wondered how I could talk with a bear who speaks several languages – including a northern Minnesota Indian language. Maybe death was not so bad. I did seek it out, right? "Who are you?"

"You wouldn't believe me if I told you," the bear answered.

I gingerly stood up, testing the stability in my legs, and throwing off the too-warm blanket. The coffee made me feel human again. A pleasantly warm breeze blew through the leaves on the trees. I turned my back to the bear. "Am I imagining you or dreaming a dream?"

"Actually, Claudia you're doing both."

"Hey, how do you know my name?"

"You're Claudia Matthews, 30 years old, a songwriter and poet. You live alone in south Minneapolis in an apartment." The bear paused for a second. "Your name is Latin and means 'lame'."

"Oh yeah, my father's idea of humor," I stammered. "How do you know this?"

"And you're a lesbian."

"What?" I could not believe my ears. Was I really hearing my life spelled out by a black bear I had met only an hour before? "Wait! You know my name, but what is yours?"

"Ursula," the bear answered.

I could not hide my smirk. "As in Ursus Americanus, your species, right?"

"Yes, precisely." If bears smiled, she did. "You're smart."

"But you're not a real bear, I mean, you look like a common black bear, but you're more than a bear." I was trying so hard not to offend Ursula.

"Yes, I'm more than a common black bear. Like you, I'm a creation of the Divine Spirit," Ursula paused, "and I'm assigned to protect you."

"You mean like, like a guardian angel?" I blurted at the peaceful-looking black bear now with wings. I blinked my eyes. Were those really wings on her back? I closed my eyes. When I opened them, the wings were gone.

"Yes, though I like to think of myself as a Spirit Guide," was her simple answer.

"Hmmmm, so that's why you rushed at me on the overlook – to protect me."

"That bullet was not meant for you." Ursula lumbered over by the fire pit and sniffed the air.

I gently sat down on the lawn chair. "But I…but I can't face this life anymore. It's too hard and I'm exhausted.

"You're badly treated, yes, but that doesn't mean it's time for you to die."

"And you know this from who?"

"The Divine Spirit." Ursula looked at me with steady eyes as big and black as, well, as a black bear's eyes. "You have so much more to do with your life and so much more to do."

I tried to shake my head, but the pain rushed back. "No, I'm a loser, a victim, a sorry-assed excuse for a woman."

Ursula growled. "Those names are from people who don't understand you."

The meek fact was amazing.

"I'm called worse," I replied. "I gave up. Can't you see that? I didn't ask for the abuse by my father or the rape by that guy in college. I didn't ask for these things…" I blurted out unable to stop myself.

Time flew back to the past, and I remembered the beatings and sexual assaults by my father. The shame and blame spread across my face as tears threatened to consume me. The pain of those events still boiled in my veins. No one ever admitted they were wrong, and that made me livid.

"I know about all those things, Claudia."

"You do?" I could feel my anger ebb. "Then, if you're my Spirit Guide, why did you let those things happen in the first place?"

"I," the answer chugged out in single words. "I can only protect you." Ursula hung her head. "Grrrrr," she roared. She grabbed a large tree branch on the ground and sunk her teeth into it. "Grrrrr!" The branch snapped in two. She turned back to me, "I'm sorry."

The apology, filled with so much tenderness, made me cry.

"I don't get it. You can protect me, but you could not stop the abuse or the rape from happening?"

Ursula returned and sat on the ground next to my chair. "No, I can't stop events that happen to you, but I can keep your father from killing you."

"But I'm dead, I shot myself, remember?"

Ursula did not answer me. She remained quiet, so I buried my face in her fur.

She was as soft as fleece and smelled fresh and clean like pine needles. I suddenly remembered hugging a teddy bear when I was four-years-old. I instantly felt like a child again protected in the presence of a mighty angel. I continued to cry with big sloppy tears.

◆◆◆◆◆

"I can keep your father from killing you." Ursula's words hung in the air like a dense fog. I closed my eyes and wondered how to respond to such honesty.

CHAPTER THREE

When angels fail to protect, children get hurt.
— Claudia Matthews

Five minutes of silence passed while the honesty of Ursula's statement threw me into a quandary. How was I supposed to respond?

"But I got hurt," I surprised myself by showing anger. This was so unlike me. I usually stifle my rage rather than let it out because I know how awful my words can be.

Ursula blinked and hung her head. "I know," she admitted. "I'm sorry."

My anger raged at what I thought was a weak answer. "Where were you when I was being attacked and abused? If you're supposed to protect me, why did you leave me in the hands of such vicious people?" I was getting started now. "When angels fail to protect, children get hurt!"

"I know," Ursula mumbled.

"This life, my life, has been one trauma after another giving me no time to recover. Here I am, 30 years old, feeling like I am still a child, feeling like I'm a complete disaster. I have no future because I have a past filled with pain and anguish. I cannot even kill myself without messing it up. Oh, how I want to bomb my past." I struggled to escape the confines of my lawn chair.

"I understand," Ursula replied.

"Do you?" I threw my words at her. "Do you really understand how awful my life has been? All that crap my father flung at me about being a freak in a circus. He said I was too dumb to achieve success in my life, and that I was unlovable. He didn't love me, and he's my father! Fathers should love their children, at least, that's what I thought they're supposed to do. Love and encourage their children, not abuse them into submission!" Big tears rolled down my cheeks.

"You're right, Claudia, your father is bound to love you."

I wiped the tears away with my sleeve. The gash in my head started to pound. I reached up feeling the blood in my matted hair. I was a mess.

A memory stirred...

At the age of 17, my father grew furious with me. He removed his black leather belt, with a large gold cross buckle, from his pant loops and whipped me until my lower back and legs burned and bled.

"I'm soooo angry!" I screamed, hurting my head and neck more. I clenched my fists, wanting to punch my father in the face. I also wanted to punch the guy who raped me. I wanted to pummel them into oblivion. Despite the pain in my neck, I kicked the dirt sending sand across the fire pit.

◆◆◆◆◆

I walked to the edge of the campsite and peered into a thick mist that covered the woods. I heard no noise from other campers or boats skimming along the river. I heard no wind in the trees or squawking birds or chattering squirrels. The air temperature was chilly, and I could smell mold in the spring grass and woods. I felt alone except for Ursula, who was watching me from her haunches.

"I'm so angry!" I yelled, carefully walking back to the lawn chair.

"You have every right to be," Ursula said adding, "you haven't done anything wrong."

"But I'm sooooo angry," was all I could muster.

"Being angry is good," Ursula raised her paw preventing me from interrupting. She continued, "You were taught that anger is bad, and the only one allowed to get angry is your father. But being angry is natural. Even animals and birds get angry. Even angels and the Divine Spirit get angry."

"The Divine Spirit gets angry?"

"Oh yes!"

"Really?"

Ursula laughed. "You know what thunderstorms are like, earthquakes, tsunamis, typhoons, and lightning. These happen when the Divine Spirit gets angry. After each of these events, peace is restored."

I thought for a moment. "But people die in earthquakes and tsunamis. Doesn't she feel guilty about that?"

"Yes!" Ursula breathed deeply. "The Divine Spirit grows angry when people stop believing and praying. She gets angry when people lose hope." Ursula tossed a small log into the fire. "Yes, people die, but the Great Spirit tries to reduce their suffering in quick ways."

I hung my head remembering how I stopped praying and hoping the world would get better. "I'm one of those people."

"Which is why you tried to kill yourself today." The statement was made without judgment.

"Yes, I want it to end. I lost hope and faith that I could get away from all the toxic people and events in my life. My life is going downhill. I see little pleasure in anything. I want to sleep for the rest of eternity." Big tears flooded my vision. It was an effort to let them roll down my cheeks. "I've lots of wonderful friends, but no one special, I'm doomed to be alone."

"No, you're not."

"And who are you to tell me that I won't be alone." I pointed my index finger at Ursula. "Who are you, really?"

"I told you I'm Ursula, your spirit guide."

"Hmmm, yes, you told me, but why couldn't you stop the abuse?"

"Have you got an hour to hear my story?"

"I'm dead, remember? I have all the time in the world."

✦✦✦✦✦

At the age of thirty, I feel like I have been living for centuries. In fact, according to a shaman I visited, I am a very old soul. My short brunette hair already has gray showing. My brothers and sisters inherited my mother's good looks while I tried to make myself look presentable. As the middle child, I felt emptiness, inadequacy, and low self-esteem. With four siblings, I did not get a lot of individual attention from my parents. In fact, most of the time, I was ignored, except for the ritual beatings by my father.

I thought my mother, Rachel Matthews Thomas, was a saint despite her lack of attention for me. She kept our household together, even though she and my father had so many kids. Mom stayed at home and did what mothers do: cook, clean, grocery shop, and shuffle my siblings and me to various sporting and religious activities. I dearly loved my mom. She was smart and pretty, and knew exactly how to make her children feel like we were special. But she also held a dark family secret, a secret she took to her grave. I shook my head to dislodge the image of Mom in her casket.

✦✦✦✦✦

Ursula coughed, drawing my attention back to her. "As you know, I'm Ursula, and presently a black bear."

"What do you mean by 'presently'?"

"I can change forms when the need arises."

"Okay, so you're a bear right now. Why did you pick this form?"

"For you." The simple answer surprised me.

"I know you like to camp and you're intrigued by bears."

"So what, I'm trying to protect myself."

"Yes. But as a child you had a small, stuffed black bear you carried with you. In fact, you'd cry and sit by the washer and dryer while the bear was being cleaned."

"Yeah, so what."

"That was me as a cub."

"You? You?" I could not believe Ursula's words.

"Yes, I've been with you for a long time."

I had heard that angels were always with you, but I did not know they could be stuffed animals. My mind exploded with possible angel forms.

"What other forms do angels take?"

"It depends," Ursula moved to the lit firepit. "Depending on the person we're assigned to, the form differs."

"Give me an example."

Ursula poked the fire with a stick. "Your sister, Emma's spirit guide, is a deer." She paused. "A very special deer?"

"Special?"

"Emma's spirit guide is an all-white deer who can run faster than the wind."

"Why the need for speed?"

"To protect Emma, her spirit guide must help her to get away fast."

"Like from our Father?"

"Right." Ursula came around the firepit and sat next to me.

"But what happens when we die? What happens to our spirit guides?"

"They're retired into the night sky and become the stars you see each night."

"There are a bazillion stars in the sky." I looked at the fire, trying to imagine all those spirit guides. "But the stars are so bright. What's up with that?"

"It's a reminder to let people on Earth know they are being watched every day and night."

"Wow, that's impressive," I paused in thought, "but then a falling star is really a falling angel, right?"

"No, angels don't fall, they retire," Ursula grunted. "There's some crazy angels that like to go zipping across the night sky for fun."

"I guess we all need some fun now and then." I grew serious. "But they fail, right?"

"Maybe in your eyes, but we spirit guides exist in the universe to protect."

"So how do you become a spirit guide?" I was beginning to enjoy Ursula's explanation even if it was hard to believe.

"I was born into an Ojibwa tribe. We were also called Chippewa, Anishinaabe, and Algonquian. Our tribe lived in what is now Ontario and Manitoba, Canada, Minnesota, and North Dakota."

Ursula paused, remembering her life so long ago. "I've always loved the forest. When I was very young I walked on a frozen pond. The ice was so smooth, I decided to skate on it." Ursula seemed lost in her thoughts. "Then, before I knew it, the ice broke, and I fell in."

"Oh my God, how awful."

"My brothers found me frozen and dead the next morning."

"How horrible!" Tears slide down my cheek. "I'm so sorry, Ursula."

"Don't be, it was an enlightening time for me. As I was drowning, I prayed to the Great Spirit. I asked her to help me protect children in my next life. The Great Spirit made a spirit guide – your guardian angel."

"What's the difference between the two?"

"Nothing. We are the same spirit."

"Okay, so what's it like to be a spirit guide?"

"Being your spirit guide is an honor. I relish the fact that I'm in your life. You're so entertaining and gifted. Your humor makes me laugh, and your lyrics make me weep."

"Seriously?" I could not believe what I heard.

"Yes, so keep writing lyrics." Ursula looked directly at me.

"But I'm dead!"

"Yes, you tried to kill yourself today. This makes a huge gap in the world."

"I doubt I have that kind of impact on the world," I mumbled through my tears.

"But you do. We all do."

"How?"

"This is difficult to explain with words. It's best that I show you." Ursula stood up to her full height. "Let's go," she grunted.

For a moment, I thought it was nuts to follow this huge creature into the woods, but what did I have to lose? My life?

Been there, done that.

CHAPTER FOUR

*We must let go of the life we have planned,
so as to accept the one that is waiting for us.*
— Joseph Campbell

I was flying, or I thought I was. I could not see the ground, and objects seemed out of focus.

"Where are we going?" I asked as the wind blew through my hair.

"Hang on," Ursula yelled back. "We're almost there."

Panic caught control of my senses, and I could feel my body shaking uncontrollably. I had no idea where we were going, and I still did not know if I was alive or dead. Nothing was normal, and the world was surreal. I could still feel my body parts, but I could not rationalize what was happening to me. I tried to sort through what I knew as fact.

◆◆◆◆◆

FACT: I remembered that I had gone to the park to kill myself. I knew I fell off the cliff, thanks to the jolts of pain in my neck and the bruises all over my body. FACT: I realized I was talking to a bear and that the bear was talking back with me about spirits and angels. FACT: I pulled my walking stick out of her shoulder, and when I did, she batted my body to the other side of the cave. Somehow we appeared in my favorite camping spot thirty-three, the campsite where I had tried to let go of my past and find a future to live toward.

I made some gains in my healing. I no longer saw my father, the very irreverent Reverend Stanley Thomas. I stopped talking to him and changed my last name to my mother's surname — Matthews. I did not want people to know that I was related to him. He was pure evil, and I needed the space away from him to feel in control of my life.

"You're so stupid," he yelled at me time and time again. "You're worthless. You're nothing but a c—." His words cut through my indifference, and I could feel the pain where he slapped me across the face. He often hit me to stop me from yelling at him, but I was not going to absorb his punishment without making my point.

But no family members ever heard my cries, or if they did, they did not acknowledge them. My father always caught me alone and forced me to do the sickest things. He shared me with a friend, Daniel, who was addicted to physically and sexually hurting adolescent girls. I threw up every time my father would take me to Daniel's house. The house was so small and smelled like bad beer and flagrant garbage.

Daniel and my father were best friends since childhood. They spent their afternoons in the forest catching and dissecting stray cats, mice, and other small animals. They laughed about the practice and thought cruelty to animals was great fun. The images they described in detail made me ice cold.

I ran away from Daniel and my father many times, but they always found me and punished me for trying to escape. Finally, after college, I left home and never looked back. I hated my father and his friend Daniel. They were sick and evil and needed to be imprisoned for life. But that was not the case because my father was a successful minister, while Daniel was a prominent businessman in Oklahoma. I considered them the 'terrible twos.'

Out of all the children in my family, I could never understand why my father singled me out. My sisters were told often enough that they were beautiful, but when it came to me, people said I was "cute." Cute was not beautiful in my mind; it was a word people used when they did not want to hurt my feelings. I often wondered if that was why my father abused me. My sisters were taller than me, and both had long red hair and firm, perky breasts. I wore my dark hair short in a kind of unruly, tumbleweed style. I always had a baseball cap on my head and was often mistaken for a boy. Flat-chested, with a love for sports, I joined the basketball team in school. Since I was short, I saw limited playing time. I was a great shooter, though, and that kept me on the team.

I had lots of friends, but I did not want them to know what was happening at home. I did not trust people except for my mom, but after years of abuse, I stopped trusting her, too. I could not understand why she stayed with a violent and abusive man. The day I realized that she could not protect herself, or me, from him, was the day I lost my heart.

There was no human in the world to protect me. Period. No mother, no father, no spirit guide, and no God.

I lost all hope that day.

◆◆◆◆◆

When I heard Ursula curse, I opened my eyes and looked around.

"Where are we?"

A dense fog surrounded everything. I was not even sure if I was walking because there was only air beneath my boots. Was I flying? Was I moving at all? I felt no wind or air on my face.

"We're almost there," Ursula finally announced.

CHAPTER FIVE

Life is filled with unanswered questions, but it is the courage to seek those answers that continues to give meaning to life. You can spend your life wallowing in despair, wondering why you were the one who was led towards the road strewn with pain, or you can be grateful that you are strong enough to survive it.

—J.D. Stroube, Caged by Damnation

When my feet finally felt like I was standing on solid ground, I opened my eyes. The sight before me was cloaked in ethereal white. Within seconds I began to see a room in some unknown medical hospital. My mother was in the bed, her face was beyond pale. I could see that she had been crying as she clutched the bedsheets around her. My father was standing on the side of her bed with an angry scowl on his face.

"If you had taken better care of yourself, this wouldn't have happened," my father said to her. More tears rolled down my mother's face.

"If your sperm wasn't so weak, our daughter would have been a healthier baby." My mother's words froze my heart.

I looked at Ursula in disbelief. "What—" I stopped.

"They can't hear you," Ursula said.

"Who are they talking about?"

"Listen."

"Oh, so you want to blame me, is that it?" my father barked.

"If you didn't drink and smoke so much, our daughter would've survived. You poisoned our daughter."

My father's hand appeared, and he hit my mother across the face. A red welt began to appear on my mother's swollen face.

I felt my body go stiff. I looked at Ursula not understanding what was going on. She directed my eyes toward the door as a nurse walked in.

"What's going on in here," the nurse demanded.

My father walked away from the bed. "It's none of your business."

"Your wife lost a baby, and she needs her rest. I'm asking you to go now and leave her alone."

"Fine," my father said and left the room.

The big-boned nurse dressed in pink plaid scrubs moved to my mother's side. "Are you all right?"

Mom nodded. "He's upset, and I made him angry. He'll be okay once he calms down."

"It's not your fault, the baby had a severe heart condition." The nurse tried to soothe my mother by plumping up her pillow.

Mom looked down at her hands. "Was there anything I could've done differently?"

"No." The nurse took my mother's hand in hers. Her deep blue eyes looked thoughtfully at my mother. "No, it was nothing that you did. If your daughter had survived, she'd have had a lifetime of heart surgeries. She chose the best path, even though it hurts you."

Mom nodded.

"Here, let me give you some medication to help you sleep. You need your rest. Things will look better once you're rested." The nurse inserted a syringe into Mom's IV and released the medicine into the tube. "There, you're going to get sleepy now. Let your body mend, and your mind will follow." The nurse left the room.

"I love you..." my mother's eyes began to close. "I love you, Claudia..."

✦✦✦✦✦

I searched Ursula's face for answers.

"I don't understand," I whispered. My throat ached, and the gash on my forehead began to throb, oh, hell it always throbbed.

"Before you were born, you were given a chance to decide whether you wanted to be a part of this family. Obviously, you chose not to." Ursula's voice was soft.

"I decided?"

"Yes."

"Do all babies have the chance to decide before they're born?"

"Yes."

"I don't understand this. You mean, we pick the family we're going to live with? We can pick a dysfunctional family or a healthy family?" I shook my head, forgetting about the pain. "You're saying that I'm responsible for picking a family with a father who beat me, abused me, and sold me to his friend?"

"It's not that simple, Claudia," Ursula waved her paw, and the hospital room disappeared in the fog. "You can decide, but the Divine Spirit must give you the tools to survive whatever path you choose."

"What tools?" I asked, my mind raced with a million questions.

"Tools like a strong physical body and the ability to bounce back after being harmed. You've always had these tools; we call them courage and resilience." Ursula's deep black eyes lightened. "You see, all humans have their own tools to survive."

"But I killed myself, remember?"

"And you had the tools to do that."

I began to shake my head, but the throbbing became worse. I held my head in my hands. "But wait!" I searched for understanding. "I didn't live. You showed me that I died in childbirth."

"What you saw was your first journey into life.

"And I didn't want to come."

"Right."

"Then I was born, so I must have changed my mind." I tried to grasp this new realization.

"You did, two years later." Ursula looked down at her paws. "That's why there's a two-year gap between you and your brother, Ben."

"But Mom never told me she miscarried."

"It was too painful for her to talk about," Ursula gently laid her paw on my hand, "she kept it to herself."

"But why would I decide to be born if I knew my father was so cruel?"

Ursula rubbed her paw on my hand. "I have an event to show you that will make things clearer for you."

◆◆◆◆◆

The feeling of flying was surreal. I did not need an airplane to propel me up into the clouds and feel the warmth of the sun on my face. I loved this feeling and did not want it to end.

"We're here," I heard Ursula say.

Enjoying the ride, I opened my eyes. "We're in a graveyard," I said quietly. "Why?"

Ursula turned toward me and said, "You need to see this." She pointed her paw to my left.

A tall dark-skinned woman, in a long gray coat, black-rimmed gray hat, black leather gloves, and sunglasses, stood before a grave. I knew she was crying since her whole body was shaking.

"Who is she?" I whispered to Ursula.

"Come closer," Ursula urged me to follow her. Ursula pointed to the grave marker. It was a small marker without flowers or a wreath.

The initials, "C. M. 1988 - 2018," were etched in the stone.

"What?" I looked at Ursula for an explanation.

Ursula nodded to my unspoken query. "This is your grave."

I sucked in my breath. When I let it out, I looked up at Ursula. "Who is this woman?"

"She would have been your soul mate, your wife."

"My wife?" I stared at the women in the gray coat. She was crying, but I could not see who it was because her handkerchief was pressed to her face.

I watched as the unknown woman knelt on the ground and ran her hand over the stone where my initials were. Then she laid a long-stem, red rose on the marker.

I could feel the tears welling up in my eyes, so I looked away because the woman's sadness pierced my soul. I felt her sorrow like it was my own. "Why was I buried here? "What happened?"

"You killed yourself, remember?" Ursula replied.

"And this is where they buried me?"

"Yes, this is a plot for people who commit suicide."

"Oh," I could feel my throat tightening. "I wasn't buried near my mother?"

"No, your father, as an evangelical minister, has the choice to bury you with official blessings or not. He did not grant you a religious ceremony."

I shrugged my shoulders not surprised by his actions. Yet the raw simplicity of my initials, birth, and death dates, seemed so stark.

"Come, it's getting late, and we have other places to go," Ursula said, steering me away from the unknown woman and my grave.

♦♦♦♦♦

The truth that no one loved me, except for the unknown woman by my grave, hit me hard. But what about my sister, Emma, who I thought loved me? And my friends from college and work?

"Suicide makes people uneasy," Ursula's words arose from the cloud we were in. "They don't understand why you were so unhappy. You never shared the dark part of your life, and so they assumed you were okay."

"I was too ashamed."

"And that's why you kept the ugly secret to yourself."

"I had to protect my siblings and my mom," I stated. "No one else would protect them."

"No one?"

"If not me, then who?" I stammered.

"The Divine Spirit and me," came the answer.

"Yeah, like the Divine Spirit protected me," I huffed.

"She did, Claudia. Your father wanted to kill you, but the Divine Spirit stopped him."

"When was that?" I countered.

"When you were 18."

My mind returned to the year 2006, but I could not remember a memory that stood out from the abuse I received.

"The Divine Spirit erased your memory of that night." Ursula looked at me with tears in her eyes. "Your mother carried that night with her forever."

I felt so weak and empty. For the first time, I was glad I was dead. I made the right decision to end the abuse. My father could never and would never touch me again. EVER!

But my mother was another story.

"Ursula, that's enough. I want to leave this place and never come back."

✦✦✦✦✦

In the next place, I knew Ursula and I were in my childhood bedroom, but it did not look like my bedroom. The furniture was the same, but the posters on the wall were different from the ones I hung. The closet door opened and my younger sister, Emma, peered out. She opened the door a little more and looked around the room. Seeing that no one was there, Emma quietly stepped into the blue bedroom. The door to the hallway whipped opened.

"There you are," my father rushed into the room and grabbed my sister by the arm.

"Ouch, you're hurting me Papa," Emma gasped, her brown eyes widening with fear.

"It's going to hurt a lot more if you don't cooperate." With one hand, he threw Emma on the bed and began unzipping his pants.

"No, Papa, don't make me do this again, please, please, Papa." Emma wiggled and tried to break free. Her curly red hair bounced around her head as she fought.

"Quiet, you know this love comes from God." He forced her to kneel on the bed. "You want God's love, don't you?"

"Yes, Papa, but not this way." Emma cried, her voice a whisper. Her shoulders sagged in surrender.

"That's a good girl," My father let go of Emma's arm. "Now, take God's blessed rod and staff into your mouth."

"But I don't want to," Emma pleaded. Tears ran down her cheeks.

My father slapped Emma across the face. "You'll do as I say. Now, put God's rod in your mouth and suck." His hips moved rhythmically forward and back. "I want you to remove your pants. God wants me to check your privates to see if you're still a virgin."

Emma did as she was told.

He removed his fingers out of Emma's vagina and placed them in his mouth. "You taste like pee, go and wash yourself. You're dirty, and you stink."

Emma slid painfully off the bed and pulled up her pants, all the while tears flowed down her face.

"And don't forget that God's love is between you and me. If you tell anyone, I promise to kill your mother."

✦✦✦✦✦

My knees buckled, and I ended up sitting on what I thought was the bedroom floor.

"Oh shit, he's hurting and abusing Emma, too." I was lightheaded and sick to my stomach. "I'm going to kill him!"

"No, Claudia, your father never touched Emma."

"But...but...you showed me that he did."

Ursula planted both her paws on my shoulders. "No. You see Claudia, in the cemetery you decided to die, so your father hurt Emma instead."

"What?" I started to shake. "You mean I'm responsible for Emma's abuse?"

"No, you aren't responsible, but he would have abused her because he didn't have you."

I pinched my eyes shut. The image of Emma being abused chilled my soul. I wanted to rake my father's eyes out with my fingernails. "How was she spared?"

"You decided to save your sister when you chose to be born."

"I did?" I could not believe what I was hearing.

Ursula nodded. "You were born to save your sister from all the pain and evil you've had to deal with. Your father would've killed Emma, so you decided to choose life and protect her."

"I—" I clenched my fists as I could still see my father assaulting my sister. "He—"

"Take a deep breath, Claudia, you're okay."

"But what happened when I left for college? Did he abuse her then?" The images that flashed through my brain left me exhausted.

"Because of you, he left Emma alone. She didn't go through the abuse you did. Fathers are not supposed to harm their kids, but then, no one is free from the book of evil." Ursula's dark black eyes suddenly grew lighter. "You saved Emma, Claudia."

"So, so if I had decided not to be born, then Emma would have been in harm's way."

"Yes. You're her protector; you've always been there for her." Ursula sat down, knowing that there were more questions that needed to be answered.

"See, I told you I had to protect my siblings. Did he hurt my other siblings?"

"No, he loved his sons and was afraid of your older sister, Judith."

"He was afraid of Judith?" I hesitated, "Why?"

"He felt she was the incarnation of the Virgin Mary. He had strong sexual feelings for her, but he didn't want to soil her."

"Soil her? What about me? He soiled me!"

Ursula gathered me in her paws and held me for a long moment. "I know, Claudia, it isn't fair, but you're the strongest in your family. None of your siblings could've lived through what he did to you. You're even stronger than your mother."

"He pushed her down the steps and killed her." All I could feel was white rage sweeping through my body.

◆ ◆ ◆ ◆ ◆

We were back at campsite thirty-three, and I felt the solid ground under my feet. I quickly sat in the lawn chair before I collapsed in shock.

Ursula heaved more logs on the fire and walked around the campsite. She played with a couple of monarch butterflies as they flew around her head. She laughed, at least I think I heard her laugh.

A deer, with completely white skin, pink ears, and nose, strolled into the campsite.

"Hi Anastasia, what are you doing here?" Ursula sauntered over to the deer.

"As I was in the neighborhood, I thought I'd say hello," the female deer answered.

"It's so good to see you," Ursula said. "What's up?"

The deer bowed her head. "Emma is traumatized."

"By Claudia's suicide."

Anastasia nodded. "She feels responsible for her sister's death."

"I'm not surprised. The two are very close." Ursula paused. "What are you doing for Emma?"

"Loving her and holding her."

"Same here."

Anastasia pawed the ground. "The Divine Spirit asks that you convince Claudia to return to the living."

Ursula scratched her head. "I know, I'm trying, but she's a strong woman who believes she's better off dead."

"Lots of people who commit suicide believe that. It breaks my heart."

"Mine, too."

Anastacia looked directly at me. "She looks like her sister."

"Yeah, she does."

The deer pawed at the dirt. "Well I should get going. I've got a lot of love to give to Emma."

Ursula nodded. "Me, too. Good to see you, Ana."

The deer bowed and disappeared into the woods.

Ursula returned to where I was sitting. "That was my friend, Anastasia. She's your sister Emma's spirit guide."

I choked on my coffee. After I cleared my throat, I asked, "Anastasia is Emma's spirit guide?"

Ursula nodded. "Yup."

"Do all my siblings have spirit guides?"

"Yes, every human does."

"Even my father?" I had to know.

"Well, he does, but his spirit guide is not from heaven."

"From hell? No shit—" I started to say but stopped. "Do all spirit guides come from either heaven or hell?"

"Yeah, the good ones from heaven and the evil ones from hell. We don't call them spirit guides, though." Ursula sat next to my chair. "They are known as Serpents of Darkness."

"That perfectly defines my father." I paused. "So there is a heaven and a hell?"

Ursula nodded again. "And then there's the place in between."

"What's that called?"

"Earth." A moment passed before she spoke again. "The Divine Spirit likes simple structures. Heaven, hell, and earth."

"But what about the other planets in the universe?"

"Those are where we spirit guides live."

"Seriously? But we call you aliens."

"I know. You humans are a peculiar bunch. Whenever you see things you don't understand you call it alien." Ursula threw another log on the fire. "Or terrorists."

"Terrorists are evil!" I stated.

"Well, that's another name for spirit guides from hell."

"Really? I get it, Ursula, I get it. There is sense in all this nonsense, isn't there?"

"Yes," Ursula laughed, "you're starting to see things as they are. Brilliant!"

A sudden thick swirling mist enveloped us. I heard Ursula's words as if in a dream.

"You need to see what really happened between your mother and father."

And then there was silence.

◆◆◆◆◆

My thoughts turned to my sister, Emma. Wonderful, funny Emma. She possessed the heart of a child and the mind of a crone. Em and I are best friends. She could make me laugh at the most trivial things people do, like the times they go through car washes with open windows. Or, people who pull away from a gas pump without removing the nozzle from their tanks.

I need to remember to tell Em that her spirit guide is an albino deer named Anastasia. She will think that is cool.

I thought of the times Em and I sat on the shore of Lake Superior. We both loved to camp, and we ventured to many of the state parks in Minnesota and Wisconsin.

Once, while Em and I were sitting on the shore, a full moon appeared casting a brilliant glow on the water. The lake was so calm that the water reflected the light like a mirror. We could not see any stars because of the brightness. The autumn air was still but fragrant with crisp fallen leaves and moss on the rocks. I remembered the beauty that surrounded us. I placed my arm around Emma's shoulders and squeezed. She was the one true light I had faith in. Em always told the truth because she got sick if she lied to anyone. Being a psychologist, her relationship with my father was formal at best.

"He's so narcissistic," Em said about my father, "he radiates in the glow of praise from the congregation. I wonder what they would think of him if they knew the truth."

"Don't bet they'll ever know."

"Oh, I believe his true nature will be revealed."

"Is that a prediction," I nudged Em.

"No, it's a gut feeling."

"You know, Em," I said, "your gut feelings have always been accurate. I think you have the gift to see into the future."

"We've discussed this a million times already." Em stood. "I'm not psychic?"

"Yeah, you are. When are you going to admit that you have a very special gift?"

"Never."

"Why, you could help so many people with your insight?"

"I don't want the responsibility. What if I made a mistake and someone gets hurt? I'd never be able to forgive myself." Em looked up at the moon.

I could see tears streaming down her cheeks. "Em, you're so kind and gentle I don't believe you could ever hurt someone."

"But what if I did? No, you call it a gift and I call it a curse." Em stood up. Her red curly hair was the color of sunsets. "I'll keep what I see to myself." She began to walk back to our campsite but stood still. Em turned to me and said, "Claudia, but I do need to let you know something."

"What is it, Em?"

"There's a skunk headed toward us and we should leave."

I gasped as the small black and white creature sauntered toward us.

"Run!" Em yelled.

And all I could do was laugh as I was running for my life.

✦✦✦✦✦

Emma. My dear Emma. Oh, how I never meant to hurt you with my death.

✦✦✦✦✦

I could hear sounds but could see nothing in the thick mist. My body felt pushed and pulled through a tunnel in a whirlwind. I heard what sounded like a washing machine. When my view cleared, Ursula and I were standing in my parents' basement.

"Let me go, Stanley. I've got to finish the laundry." Mom held a laundry basket full of dirty clothes. The scent of bleach filled the afternoon air.

I watched my mother try to get free from my father's hold. They were at the top of the basement steps.

"Stanley, dammit, let go of me," my mother shouted. She tried to wiggle out of his hold. The clothes basket fell out of her hands and bumped down the basement steps. She slapped my father across the face.

"Shut up, Rachel, you'll alert the kids," my father started to tightly wrap his arms around his struggling wife. "Shut up, will you? I've had enough of your temper today."

"Enough of *my* temper? You're having an affair with that female assistant pastor of yours," my mother spat back. "Are you beating her like you do me?"

"Rachel, I said, shut up! You sound more and more stupid. Stop fighting."

My mother stood still.

"There, that's better." My father dropped his arms to his side. He touched his jaw where an ugly red mark started to show. "Shit, you hit me!"

"And I'll hit you again if you ever lie to me again about that woman. It's over, Stan, our marriage is over." Mom tried to move, but he stepped in her way.

"It was over after the children were born, my dear Rachel. All these years you wouldn't let me touch you," he said in a ragged breath. "It's all your fault."

"My fault?"

"You never wanted to have sex, so I fucked Claudia instead."

"You what?" Mom's eyes grew wide. "You had sex with Claudia?"

"Yes, because you didn't want it."

My mother's eyes flew to my father's face. "We have five children, what do you mean we never had sex."

"We only did it so you could have children. After that, you always have a migraine or some other ailment. You put me off for years and now your brat is my sex outlet!"

"You disgusting piece of shit." My mother turned away from him but then turned back. "Not to spoil your surprise, dear husband, but I knew what you were doing to Claudia, and I filed for divorce. You'll get the papers tomorrow, and you'll lose your church and your power."

"Why you little whore!" My father's face turned beet red. The veins in his forehead began to pulsate.

"You call me the whore? NO! You're the one. You couldn't keep it in your pants." My mother's face went white. "You'll suffer for what you've done to her!"

"No one leaves me. I'm the head of this house and family. I won't agree to your divorce and that's final."

My father's right hand came out of nowhere, and he slapped my mom on the side of her head. The direct hit landed on her right ear making her sway from side to side while losing her balance on the top step.

Before I could blink, my mother collapsed and began to fall headfirst down the stairs. She tried to grab the railing, but she was falling too fast. When her head hit the concrete floor, I heard an appalling thunk. She did not move.

"Adam," my father called out my little brother's name. "Adam, call an ambulance. Your mother fell down the stairs. She's hurt." He turned away from the scene. He stammered, I didn't mean to make her fall…it was an…"

I heard my younger brother's running footsteps on the kitchen floor above us.

Adam looked down the steps and saw our mother lying in a pool of blood and dirty clothes. "MOM!" he cried, racing down with his cell phone. "MOM! Help, my mother's hurt," he screamed. "She fell down the steps and she's not breathing…please hurry…she's badly hurt."

◆◆◆◆◆

I stood next to Ursula crying and shaking. My body was trembling, and I could not make myself stop.

"I need to leave this place," I said with my mind racing and my body shaking.

"Only you know the truth," Ursula whispered. "The time for blame is over."

◆◆◆◆◆

Ursula and I sat around the fire pit at campsite thirty-three. After she built a fire, I sat nearby on a split log. The day was gray, reflecting my mood as I sat staring into the red and orange flames.

"He didn't push her."

I could not reply to Ursula's statement. My mouth was so dry, and I could hardly swallow.

"Here, drink this." Ursula handed me a steaming cup of coffee.

I kept returning to my mother's fall down the steps. She was so frail looking in her long-sleeved blue sweatshirt and blue leggings. She had been wearing a pearl necklace, but in her fall, it broke. The pearls surrounded her gray hair like dazzling stars in the dark scarlet blood.

"He didn't have to push her because he hit her," I ground my teeth. "He broke her spirit a long time ago."

Ursula nodded as she looked at me. "You brought her happiness, you know."

"I don't know how? I mean she always looked so sad."

"Not when you were around. She enjoyed your company and was very proud of your accomplishments. She saw what your father did to you physically, and surmised that he might be sexually abusing you, too. She was so indignant she sought a lawyer and filed for divorce. Claudia, your mother knew the divorce would devastate your father and ruin him."

I could feel the burn of my anger as I stood. "I asked her several times to leave him, I should've never moved away."

"When your mother found out about you she did the very best thing. She also got a restraining order against your father. Unfortunately, she died the day before he was served with the papers." Ursula began to pace. "She knew you were being abused.

Your father's confession shattered her heart. You had to move away to save yourself. Remember, he was going to kill you."

I had forgotten about this. I wanted to ask more about this, but I continued. "And almost four months after her death, I kill myself."

"Your mother is safe now. The Divine Spirit has deep compassion for abused women and children."

I turned my head to hold back the tears. I was a complete mess. I wished I had been kept in the dark about so much trauma. "What did Mom mean when she told Stanley that he'd suffer?"

Ursula looked into the sky and followed the clouds passing by. "He will suffer in the end, like all evil men do."

"Why are you putting me through this?" I spoke through clenched teeth.

"Because you need to know the truth." Ursula stoked the campfire with a stick. "The truth is always difficult to bear, yet you need to know what's real, so you can go on with your life."

I stopped listening at this point. My eyes took in a bright red cardinal singing in a tree. The notes were so sweet and somehow comforting. "Does that mean that I'm alive?"

"Does it make a difference?" Ursula shrugged her big shoulders. "What do you want to be?"

"Oh SHIT!" Rage blinded me. "Are you going to tell me it's my decision again?"

"Yes."

The wind blew through the pines swirling the smoke from the fire. I coughed when the smoke streamed into my nostrils.

"You know for being an angel you sure don't give me any clear answers. You speak in puzzle pieces – and only one piece at a time."

"Life is filled with unanswered questions, but it's the courage to seek the answers that continue to give meaning to your life," Ursula quoted author J.D. Stroube in his book, *Caged in Damnation.* She continued reciting, "And you can spend your whole life wallowing in despair, wondering why you were the one who was led towards the road strewn with pain.

"…or I can be grateful that I'm strong enough to survive it," I said finishing the quote. This quote was framed and hanging on my apartment wall.

"Yes."

"So, you know J.D. Stroube," I prodded.

"Oh, I know his writing well." Ursula agreed. "So, have you decided whether you want to be alive or dead?"

"I need some time alone. I've collected so much information. I need to think about it." I shrugged. "Is that okay? I mean, don't take it personally. I simply need—"

"It's okay, I understand. Let me know when you're ready?" Ursula said as she moved into the trees.

"Ready? Ready for what?" I yelled, but the woods had already swallowed her.

CHAPTER SIX

You are being presented with a choice: evolve or remain. If you choose to remain unchanged, you will be presented with the same challenges, the same routine, the same storms, the same situations, until you learn from them, until you love yourself enough to say 'no more,' until you choose change. If you choose to evolve, you will connect with the strength within you, you will explore what lies outside the comfort zone, you will awaken to love, you will become, you will be. You have everything you need. Choose to evolve. Choose love.

—Creig Crippen

I had no idea where Ursula was. Another dense fog descended upon me and I had no sense of time or place. My senses were dulled, I felt only emptiness, and was devoid of smell, taste, and sound.

The fog looked like the clouds I saw when I was returning to Minnesota after a trip to California. The clouds were nothing but air. I saw only white puffiness. As we descended to the runway, I saw silhouettes of houses. Once the plane landed all things came into focus.

"Welcome," an unknown voice murmured.

"Hello," my voice quivered. "Where am I?"

"You are at last in heaven."

I carefully opened my eyes to see a brilliant light shrouding over me. I looked down and saw my hands, body, and feet. I was still wearing the same clothes when I went to Banning State Park. Though the light was radiant, I could still discern silver objects like stars, moons, and other planets, although I couldn't name any. I reached out and touched a nearby star. It felt warm in my hand,

and I marveled at its texture and intricate design. The star was the finest silver I had ever seen and was woven with pure thin, blue threads. Sheer white veils floated in the air without a breeze.

"Welcome," the voice said again.

I turned my head and tried to see where the voice was coming from, but I saw no one.

"Hello," I hesitantly responded.

"Welcome, my child."

"I can't see you."

"I'm standing right in front of you, Claudia."

I peered into the light and could only see the shadowy figure of a woman. "Who are you?" I asked.

"I am the Divine Spirit," the woman said.

"So, it's true, God is a woman," I smiled suddenly thinking of Ariana Grande's popular song.

I heard the woman chuckle. "No, I'm not God. I am the Divine Spirit."

"I don't know what the difference is. Can you help me understand?"

"Absolutely."

The woman drew closer to me. Her eyes were so dark blue they reminded me of sapphires. Her skin was pure white, but I could now see her facial features slowly appearing. She was the most perfectly beautiful woman I had ever seen. I could not help but stare. She reached out and rested her hand on my chest. I could feel the heat of her hand on my heart. With that lone touch, it felt like she opened all my chakras, and I sensed immediate calm and peacefulness.

"There are many gods on Earth, but I am the source of the universe." Her comment was made without arrogance.

The Divine Spirit smiled at me. I felt immense love like the sea's waves washing over me. I giggled. "Wow, this is so difficult for me to believe. I'm actually in the presence of the Divine Spirit." A thought came to mind. "Have you heard the many prayers I said to you all these years?"

"Yes, every single one."

"Yet, you chose not to help me." I lowered my head unable to look into her eyes.

"Oh, precious child, I do help. You were never alone in your suffering. I bear your pain as if it were my own." The Divine Spirit positioned her hand under my chin and lifted my head.

"You do?" I sounded like a little girl.

"Yes, you and all humans."

"Wow! That's a lot of pain and suffering."

The Divine Spirit nodded. "I also bear all the love."

"Lucky you!" I smacked myself on the head with my hand, realizing that I sounded so immature.

The Divine Spirit chuckled again. She caught my hand in hers and suddenly, all my pain disappeared. "I love you so much, Claudia."

"Am I here to stay," I asked, feeling myself begin to shake.

"No, it is not your time."

"When?" I shook my head reeling with guilt.

"We must all work to eliminate evil, greed, and selfishness in the human heart."

"Blessed Divine Spirit, why is there evil and these other things in our world," I paused, "what meaning do they have?"

"This is a frequently asked question." The Divine Spirit looked deeply into my eyes. "All humans want to know why these things exist. When I created humans on Earth, I did so with the provision that they could live the way they wanted to. Isn't that true meaning of freedom, Claudia?"

"Yes, freedom, yes, it is," I pondered, but was still not fully understanding.

"When we are given freedom, we are given the responsibility to make choices. Some humans take this choice as an entitlement to attain everything they want, despite the outcome. Others choose to make their choices meaningful, so their actions are in humankind's best interest nurturing, nourishing, loving—all living in harmony with nature and the human soul."

"So, each one of us can be evil or good?"

"That is the ultimate choice." The Divine Spirit caught my hands in hers. "It is not a complex subject; we choose what we want from this world. Some choose evil and greed, much like your father, and others choose compassion and understanding, which is what you have chosen."

"You make this choice sound so simple."

"That's because it is. I didn't make creation so humans could fight wars, abuse children, or poison the Earth. I gave them a simple choice."

"But there are so many temptations to be bad."

"Yet, there are even more enticements to be good."

"I think I understand what you're saying." I grew quiet thinking of the huge responsibility we all carry in the decisions we make. "But with all choices there are consequences, right?"

"Yes, and those consequences are choices, too."

"So what if I choose to be evil, but then turn around and choose heaven?" I desperately cried.

"Then your actions must change to follow your choice to be in heaven." *The secret of life is love.*

When the Divine Spirit smiled, her warmth blanketed me with new understanding.

I nodded in awe. Her words sounded so simple, yet, I knew humans were complicated.

As if reading my mind, the Divine Spirit said, "Life is complicated if you choose it to be. Let me give you an example: when you feel fear in your heart is there room for love? And if you feel love in your heart, do you have room for fear?"

My mind stopped reeling. "No, of course not, yet love and fear are so powerful."

"Powerful yes, love and fear are all consuming. We return to our original reasoning behind the choices we make. Do you choose love or fear?"

"I want to choose love, so does that mean I will never fear again?"

"It depends on how much love you want to be surrounded in. Fear cannot infiltrate a sacred being of love."

"How do I become a being of love?"

"You are already a being of love."

"I am?"

The Divine Spirit wrapped me in her arms and hugged me. "Ursula will protect you and help you believe in the powers of love."

I smiled thinking of the six-foot black bear with the white tuft on her chest. "Thank you," was all I could say.

"I believe in you, Claudia." The Divine Spirit began to float back into the brilliant light.

"And I believe you."

CHAPTER SEVEN

Disappointment is considered bad. A thoughtless prejudice. How, if not through disappointment, should we discover what we have expected and hoped for? And where, if not in this discovery, should self-knowledge lie? So, how could one gain clarity about oneself without disappointment?
　　　　　—Pascal Mercier, Night Train to Lisbon

I could not overcome the fact that every time I opened my eyes, I observed myself in another location. It was no different this time when I opened my eyes. I was sitting on a flat rock perched over a flowing river. With sudden alarm, I realized this as the spot where I killed myself. I shivered. The rock below me was ice cold.

"I know you're here somewhere, but I want you to know that I deeply appreciate that you're going to help me. I believe in you, too, Ursula." I passed my fingers over the smooth cold rock.

The image of my sister, Emma, sitting on my mother's bed, began to slowly emerge. My mother was on a step stool trying to reach an object on the top shelf of her closet.

"Emma," my mother called out, "Emma, I want you to keep this for me." She hopped off the stool and handed Emma a box wrapped in a brown bag and fastened with clear tape.

"What's in it, Mom?" Emma turned the covered box in her hands. "Is it really a pair—"

"Don't open it, Emma," my mother stressed.

"But it's a pair of—"

"Shh," Mom whispered as she sat next to Emma on the bed. "It's for Claudia."

"Then why don't you give it to her?" Emma asked.

"It could someday save Claudia's life."

"What?" Emma's eyes grew wide.

"Emma, you have to trust me when I ask you to give this to Claudia if she's in trouble."

"Trouble, how?"

My mother waved her hand in dismissal. "You'll know when to give this to Claudia."

"How?"

"Emma, you have the gift of seeing things in the future."

"I don't want it," Em stubbornly replied.

"Yes, and you know you do. You received this gift from my mother." Mom took a photo off her dresser and showed it to Emma. "See, you look so much like her."

"Wow, that's me in really old clothes."

"Em, that's your grandmother. She was intuitive."

"You mean like a psychic?"

"Well, Grandma said she was intuitive. She could see things in the future like you can."

"So, what's the difference between a psychic and an intuitive?"

"An intuitive knows who's calling before she looks at her phone. When you have a feeling that you shouldn't do a particular thing on a particular day, that's intuition. If you know what a friend is going to say before they speak, that too can be called intuition."

"Okay, and being a psychic is?"

"A psychic isn't really different than a person who is intuitive. It's merely that psychics pay attention to, develop, and hone their skills. Psychic ability appears to be supernatural because so few people choose to consciously refine and actively use their intuition. Anyone can work to develop their psychic abilities, although some people are naturally gifted in this way, like others are natural musicians or athletes."

"But I don't want to be either psychic or intuitive."

"You have no choice, you already are!" My mother stroked Em's cheek. "And you need this gift to protect people."

"Like who?"

"Whom," Mom corrected.

"Like whom?"

"Like your sister and best friend, Claudia."

Realization spread across Emma's face. She nodded. "You mean I got this from my Grandma?"

"Yeah, and she used her gift to help people when they were in trouble." Mom wrapped her arms around Em. "I watched Grandma save a young boy's life."

"How?"

"Your Grandma saw into the future like you can. She saw that a young boy in the neighborhood was going to get hit and killed by a brown car. So, on that day she stopped the boy on the corner and asked him to help her across the road."

Em's eyes grew wide. "Then what happened?"

"By asking for his help, the boy stepped back onto the curb as the brown car raced by."

"She also predicted that President John F. Kennedy would be assassinated on November 22, 1963."

"She did? Wow!"

"And that's what you want me to do with Claudia and this box. Save her?"

"Yes, if Claudia's in trouble you need to give her this box, but not before."

"How will I know?"

"Oh, honey, you'll know when it's the right time. Please trust your gift."

Emma nodded again.

My mother started to cry.

"Mom, why are you crying. Is something going to happen to you?" Emma's brown eyes searched my mother's tear-streaked face. "You're leaving us, aren't you?"

Through her tears, my mother smiled and nodded. "Don't worry about me, worry about yourself and Claudia, okay?"

"Claudia needs my help?"

"Yes, and you need to give her this box when it's time." My mother stood. "Emma, please remember that I will always love you."

Emma hugged Mom as tears streamed down both their faces. "I love you, too, Mom."

◆◆◆◆◆

I shook my head. "Great! Now I'm seeing things without Ursula."

I stood up on the rock to shake the scene out of my neck and shoulders. When I did, I winced but there was no more pain. Where was Ursula anyway? And what was in the box?

◆◆◆◆◆

"You said that babies can choose before they're born, whether they want to be born or not, right?" My question to Ursula rushed back.

"Yes."

Suddenly, Ursula disappeared, and I saw Emma standing in front of me. She was smiling, winked, and said, "I decided to be born because I knew you'd protect me, and I'm so grateful." Her red curls moved around her shoulders as she approached me and wrapped her arms around my waist. I suddenly felt a burst of warmth race through my body. When I looked at Emma, she suddenly began stepping away. "I still need you to protect me, Claudia. I need you to come back."

Her request hit me hard, *"I need you to come back."*

I quickly sat down on the rock because I knew I would fall if I did not. My knees were shaking. I wrapped my arms around my knees and hugged them until they stopped moving. Emma's words clarified for me that I did, indeed, need to fight back.

◆◆◆◆◆

My snoring woke me, which made me wonder if dead people could snore. I shrugged my shoulders, "Well, I guess I can snore when I'm dead."

◆◆◆◆◆

Being dead is a quirky kind of presence. I mean, it is an end but not really. Everywhere I look, I see the most beautiful planet. The pine trees are taller and greener in color. The sky is a blue that does not exist on our color charts. I guess that is why they call it heavenly blue. The clouds are puffier and whiter, the water in the lake is perfectly clear with a silver tint. I see deer, squirrels, and raccoons wandering around without fear. Is this how I pictured heaven? No, I do not remember ever having a vision of heaven.

The version of heaven my father described was so unreal. He painted a picture that heaven was a great mansion where God sat on a throne of gold. He wore a gold crown sprinkled with dazzling colored gems. The elegant mansion had many rooms and was filled with dark blue silk flags bearing silver planets on each one. The floor was polished marble, and the doors were made of shiny bronze. Large yellow, white, and red pillows were on the floor where souls eagerly gathered to hear the word of God. I washed this image from my mind.

This was certainly not my idea of heaven. I now possessed a more perfect picture of heaven, and I intended to hold the purity in my heart forever.

I stepped down to the lake and as I stood in the water, my boots did not even get wet. I looked for a glimpse of my reflection. There I was bending over and looking like hell. My hair was a brownish-gray mess, and I saw where the bullet grazed my forehead above my left eyebrow, still a dark red. I raised my hand to feel it. The wound still hurt, which surprised me, because I guess I had not thought in heaven, you could feel pain. *But I thought the Divine Spirit healed my pain?*

I laughed to myself realizing I did have an image of heaven.

"You're not in heaven," said a voice behind me. I whirled around and saw Ursula standing on the shore.

"Oh, you're back. What do you mean I'm not in heaven?"

"This isn't heaven." Ursula kneeled on her paws and peered into the lake. She suddenly jerked her paw up with a bright-colored walleye and swallowed it in the same motion.

"Nice catch."

"A girl has to eat," she said, extracting fishbones from her mouth. She waded deeper into the water and repeated the same motion. Another big walleye was in her grasp. She ate it and removed the fishbones.

"I'm not hungry." My words sounded like a pout.

"That's because the dead don't eat." Ursula stood up on her back paws and walked out of the water. Unbelievably, her fur was dry.

"Ha, so I am dead!"

"Technically, no, you're in a holding space for people who must decide whether they want to be alive or dead."

My eyes grew wide. "You mean I can choose if I want to be alive or dead?"

"Like babies do." Ursula plopped on the sand and rolled over on her back. She began to wiggle in the sand, scratching her back. "Ah, I love this."

"Don't get sand in your wound, otherwise it's going to hurt."

"I'm healed." Ursula stood up and shook the sand off her fur. She lumbered toward me and showed me her shoulder. It was completely healed.

"How can your wound be healed but mine isn't?"

"I'm an angel, and you aren't."

"So how do I become an angel like you?"

"The Divine Spirit decides whether or not you have the qualities to be an angel."

"Sounds like a job interview," my sarcasm dripped.

"You think this is funny." Ursula turned away and started for the trees.

"Wait," I called out, "Wait, Ursula," I ran after her. "I'm sorry, I don't understand what happened at Banning and why I'm here."

Ursula stopped and perched on an old oak log. She motioned for me to come closer. "Sit."

I did as Ursula said. "Ursula, I saw the Divine Spirit."

"I'm well aware of your visit to her. But, getting back to the here and now, you still drove to the park to kill yourself, and you did." Ursula waited for a response. When there was not one, she continued. "No, the bullet didn't kill you, but the fall from the cliff did. You broke your neck on the rocks."

I reached behind me and felt my neck. There was lots of pain. "How?"

"I arrived in time to prevent the bullet from going through your brains, and then we tumbled over the cliff together. As we fell, I managed to get behind you, but I couldn't protect your head. That damned walking stick of yours fell with us and pierced my shoulder."

I looked down feeling shame course through my body. "I'm so sorry I, I, I didn't mean to hurt you."

"Yes, you did. You thought I was a ferocious animal."

"But you were."

Ursula suddenly stopped herself and laughed. "You're right, but I was running to save you."

"And I thought you were an attacking bear. I thought you were going to eat me."

"I told you I'm a vegetarian, remember?"

"I never thought angels were vegetarians," I said.

"You have a limited view of heaven," Ursula stated. "Your father's description is way off."

How so?"

"Heaven is a place of unconditional love, a place of extreme quiet and ultimate peace, and a place of truth." Ursula bowed her head.

"Unlike our Earth?"

"Yes, very. In heaven there's a spot for all souls who want to reach the pinnacle of innocence and wisdom. There is no darkness in heaven."

"I know the light is blinding," I mumbled. "So, what exactly do souls do in heaven?"

"They pray and meditate."

I stretched and pondered Ursula's description of heaven. It seemed like the perfect place to exist. Then I asked Ursula, "Am I your first case?"

"My first case? I don't know what you mean."

"Your first angel case?"

Ursula looked at me and then looked away. "That obvious, huh?"

She looked so embarrassed the sight made me laugh. I could not stop myself, and soon we were both laughing.

"Yeah, I'm in training. You weren't supposed to fall off the cliff. My orders were to prevent you from shooting yourself."

I pointed to the gash on my forehead and to my neck. In response, Ursula pointed at the shoulder my walking stick pierced.

"Okay, we're even then. You saved me, and I saved you."

"Well," Ursula suddenly turned serious. "I haven't saved you yet. You're still deciding whether you want life or death."

"Oh, yeah, I guess I forgot about that little detail." I stood up and leaned against the trunk of a pine tree feeling the solid mass behind me.

"Look Claudia, you've been through a lot in your 30 years, and I know you want to stop the pain and the horrible memories. Your father is evil, and he will pay for what he has done to you, your mother, and your family." Ursula sighed. "But there's still something you have to do."

"I do?"

"Yes." Ursula's eyes squinted. "You have to go back and confront your father for his deeds."

"I WHAT?"

"You've got to go back and confront your father with the truth."

I gasped for air. My mind ran at warp speed. My memories of being burned with cigars and a broken bone protruding from my sleeve returned in full force. When vile images swirled around in my head, I felt sick. I vomited by the pine tree. "I can't do that." My voice was weak.

Ursula walked over to me and handed me a red bandana. It was moist, so I washed my mouth and tried to spit out the last taste of vomit.

"I'm really sad to say this, but then you are, indeed, dead."

"What?" I could find no more words to say. A fluid chill overtook my body. Once again, I lost all sense of time and place. I could only feel the chill burn my head, back, arms, and legs. When the chill reached my heart—I knew my life was over.

CHAPTER EIGHT

Insanity is doing the same thing over and over again and expecting different results.
—Albert Einstein

Ursula sat in silence and refused to look in my eyes. I was frozen where I stood and could not move. Finally, as the snow began to fall again, she began.

"You've experienced much in your lifetime. Some of it is so horrendous it breaks my heart. You continue to survive, even though you don't want to. You've asked for death, and yet you refuse to see the beauty you've created in your life."

Ursula continued.

"Yes, your heart has been ripped out of your chest, and your eyes have seen the world's darkest moments as a child. Your ears have heard the screams from hell. Your hands have grasped empty air, and yet your arms carry the burden of so many lost childhoods."

Her gaze pierced my soul.

"You aren't done yet, though; you want to let your spirit go. I ask that you go back and find the child in you and comfort her. Love her and show her the gift of survival. Help her turn her dreams to fruition. Give your heart to her and love her—love her with all your bones, muscles, cells, and flesh. This child is you, and you must save her."

◆◆◆◆◆

Anger exploded from my heart in rays of searing fire. My chilled body thawed and felt raw to the reality that now faced me. I knew this was the moment that I needed to face my demons.

"I do not believe that I was able to choose my family before I was born. What type of lunatic would I be to pick this family? This responsibility is too overwhelming, too complex for the simple and innocent mind of an infant. The truth is I was born wounded. Period. I was born in a world filled with darkness, evil, and suffering. It's always been this way from the very beginning of time. We live…we suffer…we die.

I did not choose to be born a victim or a crime statistic. I thought I was born to absorb and reflect the balance I see in nature. A tree grows, a tree dies. The balance keeps our Earth from falling out of the sky, or the sun from exploding.

I was born to discover balance and harmony in a culture rooted in cruelty. I am pure energy, and this energy must be used to heal the wounds of a world so divided and separate. I am light and goodness. Period.

Yet, I did not ask for the wars or disasters, disease, or destruction. In my simple child brain, I never dreamed that man could be so dangerous and so deadly. Man has slaughtered the beasts, poisoned our oceans, and polluted the air. This is not why I came here, yet, this is what I face every day. I could say that it is not fair but man does not care. All I see is epic greed, a lust for money, and immense power. We go insane trying to understand the inevitable, that our Earth is dying and when the Earth dies, we all die.

If I cannot save myself, then how can it be my responsibility to save civilization? We humans live and we die. How will my life be measured and how will the good I have done be remembered?

I was born wounded. The abuse did not start with me; it started generations ago, generations of shame and horror.

I am living proof of what dysfunction looks like, and my survival is based solely on my attempts to ignore and forget the darkness. I now know that I suck at committing suicide, unlike so many of my ancestors who successfully killed themselves in the wake of sheer malice. I know now that I am to open the past and reveal this ugly truth: to witness the horrific and give voice to the damaged. I am not a healer because I cannot push away the decades of hatred for my female ancestors, nor can I brush aside their tears. We are not property to be sold and enslaved. We are not the souls who were tied to stakes and burned. We are not the women who must be constantly bullied, harassed, and exploited for the pleasure of men.

I am a woman born to nourish life, not destroy it.

I do not hate men, and I chastise myself for creating the belief that all men are evil. Men need women, and women need men, but that is not one singular equation. Love does not divide. To bring balance into our world, we must share our experiences with each other, and live united in communities of peaceful balance.

Though the burdens in life are many and the moments of peace few, I look to myself to hear the voices of my ancestors who plead to be rescued and receive unconditional reconciliation.

I was born wounded, but I chose to be born. I choose this life not for simplicity but for the insurmountable challenges. Where will I fill my empty heart? Where will I find the one true peace? I have the right to ask where the answers are as well as the hope because without this hope and peace, I am nothing.

I am here today with my ancestors, both women and men, who cry out to stop this madness. I hear their pleas. I feel their suffering. I am part of them. I am their future. I am their hope.

"Yes, I am their hope."

◆◆◆◆◆

Ursula and I are again sitting in silence as the chilly wind continues to blow. Snowflakes swirl around us as if we are in a snow globe. The location where we now sit is cloaked in an eerie shimmering whiteness. Both of us, Ursula and I, are lost in our thoughts. We are somewhere else until a red cardinal lands on a log between us. The cardinal looks at each of us, lowers its head, and lets out a cry so sorrowful I start to cry.

"Your ancestors are here, Claudia. They want you to know that you have their support." Ursula was tearful, too. "They'll be with you as you end the abuse. They only ask that you trust them, that you place your love and faith in them to help you. You're not alone, Claudia, please remember this, you're never alone."

I could not speak. Finally, after what seemed like hours, I asked Ursula, "Will you be with me?"

"Yes, always." The cardinal flew to a branch and continued to watch us.

I stood up and looked at the cardinal and then at Ursula. "My mother always loved cardinals and when I see one, I can't help but think of her."

Ursula nodded.

"Is Mom here with us?"

"Yes," came the simple reply.

"Okay, then I'm ready. I'll go back with the knowledge that you, Mom, and my ancestors are with me. Please give me the tools I'll need."

Ursula nodded again.

When the white light slowly faded, I was wrapped in darkness.

CHAPTER NINE

It is not the strongest species that survive, nor the most intelligent, but the ones most responsive to change.
— Charles Darwin

I could smell blood, but I could not open my eyes. Ice cold water was thrown in my face and I jerked up into a sitting position. Dark black boots stood before me. They were the only objects I could see from the slits in my eyes.

"You are intensely evil, girl!" My father's voice filled my senses. "There is no hope for you." He crouched down to glare into my face and forced my head up with his hand. His breath smelled of beer. I knew immediately he was drunk and angry, but I had no idea why. "So, you hate men? That's the rumor going around town. People say you like women instead, that you eat pussy." I heard him unzip his pants. "I'll teach you to worship the rod, God's gift to women."

He ripped off my underwear with his big hands, knelt between my legs and forced them apart. I cried out from the pain of his entry.

"God's given me a demon to save, and I must salvage your soul from the evil women in this town. They don't belong here and neither do you. Tell me how much you like God's rod, girl."

"I don't," I managed to voice before he slapped me hard across the face. "I don't love your little penis."

Another slap and I felt myself suddenly escape my body, and from high above the ceiling, I watched what he was doing to me. My face was horribly bruised, my nose and lips were bleeding, and my left arm lay beside me at an awkward angle. The door to the basement suddenly flew open and my mother came rushing down the stairs.

"Stanley, no!" she shrieked. "For God's sake, stop!"

He rose from the floor, turned his back to his wife, and fastened his pants. "She's a lesbian, Rachel, a woman-fucking-woman." He turned and spat on me.

My mother was shaking and crying and did not see my father's naked penis before he stuffed it into his pants. Mom had been looking at me since coming down the stairs seeing only my broken arm. "Stan, I need to bandage her arm, it's broken." She stood between my father and me. He shrugged her off but then looked at my arm. For a moment, it appeared that he realized what he had done.

He brushed past my mother with an angry scowl, walked up the steps, and slammed the basement door behind him.

When I returned to my body the pain came over me like a tidal wave. I could not even cry, but the pain made me moan.

"Shhh, dear, I'm here and I'm going to get you some medicine to get rid of the pain, but first I have to wrap your arm." She looked around and saw a bedsheet in the laundry basket. She ripped a piece off and found a small board leaning up against Father's workbench. She carefully tied the sheet around my arm and the wood. "I'm so sorry, Claudia, I'm so sorry he did this to you."

"It's not the first time, Mom. After living through 17 years of his maliciousness, he can break my bones, but he can't hurt me."

My mother stopped the wrapping, sat back on her heels, and stared at me. Her brown eyes were wide. "He's done this to you before?"

I nodded and said weakly, "You know he's been doing this to me all along."

"When did he start doing this to you?" she asked, ignoring my comment as she tightened the knot.

"I don't remember, but I think I was eight or ten."

"But you were so young," my mother said as anger shot through her. "I'm sorry, baby, I'm so sorry." She stood and reached out her hand to help me up. "Let's get some ice on your face, okay?"

"Okay," I said as I tried to stand. "I hate him!"

"Shhh, dear, you're in pain, and you don't know what you're saying. Let's get you some medicine. Come on," she led me to the stairs. "He doesn't know what he's doing when he drinks."

Yes, he does," I thought.

CHAPTER TEN

The rain falls because it can no longer handle the heaviness. Just like tears, they fall because the heart can no longer handle the pain.
—Anonymous

I knew immediately my wellbeing was terribly amiss. I could not move my legs or arms. I lay on a soft surface, but I felt like I was strapped down.

"Now, now," a female's voice said. It wasn't my mother's voice, "You shouldn't try to move. You've been badly hurt."

I opened my eyes and saw a nurse at the side of my bed. She was putting a syringe into an IV bag.

"This will make you more comfortable," she said smiling.

"Where am I?" My question was answered with a pounding headache.

"You've been hurt," the nurse said as she tried to comfort me.

"My father did this," I screamed, but the pain in my neck and back made me stop. The room seemed to tilt.

"No, no, Miss, your father didn't do this." She looked away as another woman in a white coat came into the room. Her name tag said, Dr. Lisa Lewis.

"Hello Claudia, I'm Dr. Lewis and I'm the physician treating your injuries."

"What happened?" My throat burned.

"You injured your neck. We're still running tests to see how bad it is, or how good as I like to think of it." She turned on her flashlight and shined it in each of my eyes. Then she examined my forehead and the gash. She turned to the nurse and said, "She's got a low-grade temp; let's see if we can bring that down. It'll make her more comfortable."

The nurse nodded and removed another syringe from the drawer near my bed. She inserted it into the IV and squeezed the contents into the tube. "There, you should feel that nasty headache going away in a little bit."

"The gash in your forehead will heal, but I'm afraid your hair won't grow back there." Dr. Lewis said as she replaced the bandage. "Can you tell me what happened?"

"I...I was down in the basement and my father; well my father was very angry with me..."

Dr. Lewis touched her index finger to her lips. "That's okay, you rest now. You're a bit confused and we can talk about what happened later." The doctor wrote something in a chart. "Try to rest and don't move your head, okay?"

I tried to nod, but pain shot through my neck again. "Can you tell me something?" I reached out to the doctor with my eyes.

"Sure," Dr. Lewis replied.

"Am I dead or alive?"

The doctor leaned in over my bed. "You are gratefully alive, my friend."

◆◆◆◆◆

"You are gratefully alive, my friend."

The doctor's words kept running through my mind. I was so confused that I made the doctor's sentence a mantra, chanting it repeatedly trying to believe that I was alive and safe in a hospital bed.

The medication the nurse gave me was a blessing from the excessive pain, but it also made me feel like I was floating on a cloud again. Yet, as the drug began to wear off, my head was squeezed into a vice that kept getting tighter and tighter. I may be alive, I thought, but I am in a living hell.

"Good morning, Claudia," Dr. Lewis said as she entered my room. "How are you feeling today?"

"Much better than I did yesterday."

"Oh, you mean three days ago. Good." She perused my chart. "Your collarbone is broken and your neck was damaged in your fall, which means you damaged other parts including your bones, joints, soft tissue, and nerves that work together to hold up and move your head." She turned the page and continued, "Your treatment depends on a lot of factors including your age, other medical conditions, and the extent of damage to your spine. Luckily, you didn't fracture your neck, but I want you to wear a halo brace for eight weeks.

"What's a halo brace?"

"A metal brace that circles and attaches to your skull. It's used to keep the bones in your cervical spine and neck from moving. Pins screwed into the skin above your eyebrows keep the halo in place. Metal rods connect the halo to a plastic vest worn over your chest and back."

"Sounds gruesome."

"Yes, but it's very effective," Dr. Lewis added.

"How long do I have to wear it?"

"Eight weeks."

"Two months? Wow, that's a long time."

"Yes, but it would've been worse if you had fractured your neck," Dr. Lewis smiled. "You're a lucky woman. Your guardian angel was working overtime to keep you safe."

"Hmmm, yes, my guardian angel." It was the first time that I thought of Ursula. I felt guilty.

◆◆◆◆◆

So, I am back and alive. Ursula never told me I would return to the living injured. Now it made sense to me why my neck hurt so much. I did hit the rocks! Ursula said that she tried to move behind me, but was unable to at the rate we were falling. But she did prevent me from fracturing my neck, though I did break my collarbone. I closed my eyes.

"Thank you, Ursula," I whispered. I waited for a response but heard only silence.

Having been in Ursula's presence for only a short time, I was amazed at how much I missed her. She showed me truths that I never comprehended, and yet continued to be so vague that it drove me nuts. Is this how angels talk? They give you some of the story but not everything. I guess I am meant to find out the truth on my own. Oh, how easy life would be if she told me all about my present life and future.

Ursula directed me to a hospital so that I could recover from my injuries, both self-inflicted and not. The pain was real and so were the consequences of my actions. I felt guilty for inserting myself in harm's way. I could look past where the bullet grazed my forehead, but I had to accept the fact that I careened off the cliff, hurting my neck. My temporary paralysis was my responsibility. I could no longer ignore the facts. I attempted and failed to end my life, and now I had to take responsibility to heal my body and mind.

The facts were vividly clear. FACT: I have been abused physically, sexually, and psychologically by my father. FACT: I did not believe in tomorrow because I saw no hope in the future. FACT: I was a coward taking the beatings rather than standing up for myself and fighting the abuse. FACT: I have never talked about what was happening at home to people who could have helped me. FACT: I hated myself for not standing up for me. FACT: I tried suicide to escape my troubles rather than seek help. FACT: I needed to begin living all over again.

I needed to begin living all over again.

I could feel tears streaming down my cheeks in rapid succession. Before I met Ursula, I believed I was alone, but now I knew she was here for me, not physically but, definitely, emotionally and spiritually.

Now was the time for me to make a change, a huge change…I promised myself.

◆◆◆◆◆

"Hey, Sis," Emma said as she walked through the door. Her big smile brightened the room. "They finally let me in to see you. I guess they don't allow a lot of visitors in the psych ward." She winced and placed a stuffed black bear on my stomach. "I thought you needed something to hug while you're wearing that brace."

"Thanks, Em," Smiling to myself, I tried to reach the bear, but I couldn't raise my arms. "It's good to see you."

"And it's so good to see you, Sis."

Emma looked out the window of my hospital room and shifted her weight on one foot, then to the other. I knew this was her way of letting me know she was anxious and did not know what to say.

"I know this is really awkward, Em, but how did I end up here?"

"I stopped by your house the morning of the snowstorm."

"How long ago was that?" I asked, suddenly wanting to know the date.

"A week."

"A whole week?" I tried to move but my head was held down.

"Yeah, you've been in and out for a week."

"What happened?"

"The voices I hear warned me you were in danger. When you didn't answer the doorbell, I knocked and then checked to see if your car was in the garage. When it wasn't, my senses started spinning. I knew you were in trouble, so I called the police and reported you missing." Emma bit her nails.

"Stop biting your nails."

"Oh, sorry," Emma's eyes were brimmed with tears. "I told the police that I thought you traveled to Banning. They discovered you there half alive." Her voice quivered.

"Oh, Emma, I'm so sorry I did that to you."

Emma nodded. "According to the State Troopers, it was a weird scene."

"What do you mean by weird?"

"Well, when the State Troopers reached the park, they saw a black bear dragging you to your car." She sniffled. "They almost shot the bear, but it looked hurt. Then she let go of you and wandered off."

"A bear?"

"A big black bear. It didn't bite you, thank God. The troopers hauled you out of the park and transported you to the hospital." Her big brown eyes filled with tears. "I was so afraid you were going to die." She wiped away her tears with her sleeve. "I'm here for you, you know."

"You're the only one in the family who is." I watched as Emma's shoulder-length red curls bobbed slowly as she nodded.

"It's been so hard on all of us, what with Mom dying and now your accident." At the age of 27, Emma was a spark plug. Always the realist and always the sweetheart of the family. I didn't know anyone who wasn't charmed by her—me included.

"I know, Em. I'm sorry. You're not to blame for what I did, so don't feel guilty."

"But I do. I know Father has treated you so badly, and I've never stood up to him on your behalf."

"I'm glad you didn't. He would've hurt you, too, and badly."

The tears appeared again in Emma's eyes. She swallowed a sob and when she gripped the side rails on my bed with both hands, her knuckles turned white. I could see she wanted to say more but didn't. "I wish he had died instead of Mom."

I could not suppress my own tears as they cascaded down my face.

"Hey, listen, I didn't mean to visit and make you feel bad. I should leave and let you rest." Emma removed her hands from the bed railing.

"Will you come back and see me?" I asked, so afraid to be alone.

"Yes. I love you, Claudia."

"I love you, too, Em," I said as my tears continued to fall.

◆◆◆◆◆

In my heart, I knew it was time to explain to Dr. Lewis, and Dr. Sloan, the psychiatrist assigned to me, what happened on the day of my "accident," the term the hospital gave to my suicide attempt. Dr. Sloan was a small petite woman with white hair and the most soulful green eyes.

"Can you tell me what happened?" Dr. Sloan's voice was soft but powerful.

"I…I…I wanted to end my life." I had to take a deep breath. "When my Mom died, the pain in my heart grew so unbearable. I couldn't live like this. I left for the state park to kill myself." I looked away and out the window. Telling the truth was going to be depressingly complex.

"Claudia," Dr. Lewis, who was also in the room, gently asked, "have you been physically and sexually abused?"

I tried to nod, but the halo brace kept me from doing so. "Yes."

"Who has been abusing you?" Dr. Sloan already knew, but she added, "your mother, your father?"

"Oh, no, my mother would've never done anything to hurt me. She was the one who took care of my cuts and bruises."

"So, it was your father then?"

"Yes."

"How long has he been hurting you?" Dr. Sloan made a note on her yellow-lined pad of paper. "Do you remember when he started to hurt you?"

"I don't remember how early it started, but it became sexual between the age of thirteen and fifteen."

Dr. Lewis looked at Dr. Sloan, but they remained silent.

"Claudia, since you've been here in the hospital, we had to do a series of tests on you including a full-body scan. We discovered several places where you have bone remodeling, most in your arms and legs. Were you treated by medical doctors for these breaks?"

"Some." I paused trying to remember. "My mother sometimes straightened my bones and kept them wrapped until I could use my arm again. She'd give me a sip of some awful drink before she touched my broken bone, and then gave me some more of that awful drink."

"You've suffered a lot of injury and pain in your young life," Dr. Sloan stated.

"Yeah, but the broken bones kept my father from hurting me for a while. Sometimes he didn't touch me for months while I was able to heal."

"I see." Dr. Sloan mumbled as she made another note on her pad of paper. "Did your father break any bones of your brothers or sisters?"

"No." I saw both doctors sigh.

"Has your father ever been arrested for hurting you and your mother?"

"No. He told his congregation he had a child possessed by Satan, and that he asked for the hand of God to heal us."

"So, he's a minister?" Dr. Lewis asked the question this time.

"Yeah, unfortunately."

"How did your mother die?"

"She fell down the basement steps. I thought at first that he pushed her, but then I saw what really happened."

"How did you see this?" Dr. Sloan looked up from her notes.

"I...well...I saw it in...when, when...I had a dream." I remembered I was in a psych ward and that I should be careful about telling what I experienced between life and death. "I had a dream," I repeated.

"Did you have any other dreams?" Dr. Sloan asked.

"No, no I haven't had any for a while," I said quickly but I could see from the doctors' faces that they knew I wasn't telling the truth.

"Why don't we stop for the day. Claudia, I think you could use a rest at this point. You've been through a lot." Dr. Sloan sympathetically peered at me and then at Dr. Lewis. "Wouldn't you agree, Dr. Lewis?"

"Yes, absolutely." Dr. Lewis turned to me. "Claudia, do you need some pain medication, you look really pale?"

"No, that's okay. I want to sleep because I'm tired."

◆◆◆◆◆

The halo brace was a super pain. The screws were drilled into my head to prevent me from moving my head. It was extremely uncomfortable, but as Dr. Lewis explained, the brace was necessary to return the full range of motion in my neck.

Dr. Lewis also prescribed an antidepressant to help me cope with my nightmares and flashbacks. She said it would take several weeks before the medication would have an effect. I prayed that it would be sooner rather than later. I hated feeling so hopeless all the time. Being bedridden, I found myself going back to Hell's Gate and wishing the outcome had been different.

Why Ursula didn't tell me that my neck was so damaged, I did not know? And why did she not tell me I would be bedridden with a halo brace? Probably, I thought, she knew if I knew this was going to happen, I would not have agreed to come back.

Through the following weeks my body was healing and growing restless, but my neck was taking its time. I asked one of the nurses if she could bring in a mirror so I could see what the brace looked like. I did not want to know at first, but my curiosity got the better of me. What I saw in the mirror terrified me.

My face was bloated and my forehead had a nasty gash where the bullet had grazed my skin and hairline. Now that it was healing, the gash looked like a walking stick. Okay, it really did not look like that, but I imagined it did. The scar reminded me of Ursula, and for the second time since coming back to life, I missed her terribly.

With my hands shaking, I managed to pick up and hug the stuffed bear Emma had given me. "Oh, Ursula, I know you can hear me. I miss you." I swear the stuffed bear smiled at me. "I don't know how I'm going to deal with my father when I'm bedridden."

◆◆◆◆◆

I was sleeping when I heard my name called.

"Claudia, Claudia, it's your father," he said again.

I prayed I was dreaming. I opened my eyes but quickly closed them.

"I know you can hear me, girl," he said in his typical rough way.

"What do you want?" I looked straight into his eyes.

"I came to see how you are."

"Well, you can tell I'm not doing very well." My body froze into defensive mode.

"Yeah, you really pulled off your suicide attempt." He smirked. "You couldn't even do that right."

"Go away."

"Hell no, this is too much fun. I finally have your full attention unlike when you were a child." He moved closer to the bed.

I could feel my body stiffen.

"Nice halo, though you'll be wearing horns for the rest of eternity." As he grabbed the brace, I tried to pull away.

Sheer pain shot through my head, neck, and shoulders. "Don't touch me." Tears filled my eyes.

"I came to say a prayer for you and this is how you treat me, you, ungrateful slut." He reached into his suit jacket and pulled out his clerical stole. He kissed the vestment and placed it around his neck.

"I don't need nor want your prayers."

"Oh, yes you do. You are a sinner, and you need to ask God to forgive you for trying to prematurely end your life. You need to know that God is very angry with you."

I could smell beer on his breath, and it made my stomach turn. I had not seen him since my mother's funeral and suddenly saw how frail he looked. His gray hair and beard were unkempt and his suit was wrinkled. He probably slept in it.

"Your God is angry, and I don't believe in him. I believe in a Divine Spirit that outranks your God."

"How blasphemous! Girl! You are going straight to Hell." His face turned a deep red.

"No, you are. In fact, I've seen your ticket and it's a one-way ticket. You're never going to be able to return to this life."

He brought his face close to mine. His eyes were dilated like that of a crazy person's. My nerves began to prickle with fear.

"Dear God, forgive this child for her sins. She has spent her life doing evil and partaking in the pleasures of the flesh…"

I laughed which only made him turn redder in the face. Now his hands were shaking.

"…with her own sex. She is not worthy to receive you, but I ask for your patience with her. She will return to you, oh Lord, and commit her life to doing good work. She needs and wants your forgiveness."

"No, I don't."

He stopped praying, and I could tell he was trying to contain his anger. He leaned closer to me.

"All mighty Father, please continue to teach her the true lessons that will free her soul from Hell."

"Been there, done that," I smiled even though my body was on high alert. I wish I could have involuntarily passed out at that moment. I wanted him to go away.

"Great Father, I, your humble servant, ask that you forgive this child for her sins and send her on a journey where she will follow you and worship you."

"Not going to happen," I added.

"She is sick in heart and soul and needs to be punished for her blasphemous words and thoughts. I ask you to give me the strength to show her your love."

Before I could react, his hands reached out and jerked my brace sideways. A hurricane of pain cruised through my whole body.

"DAMN IT!" I cried out.

"What's going on in…" a nurse demanded as she rushed into the room. "What are you doing?" She flew at my father and grabbed his hands off my brace. "You, you need to leave at once."

My father stood there refusing to let go of the brace.

"I said let go or I'll call security!"

He gave my brace the slightest tug and released his hands.

"Out!" The nurse sternly said, "And don't come back."

My father turned toward the nurse and said unperturbed, "Listen, this is my daughter, and I'll do what I want with her.

"Not under my watch, you won't," the nurse grasped my father roughly by the arm and led him to the door. "Don't come back, Mister."

"That's Reverend," my father spewed out.

"Like I said, don't come back Mister Reverend."

When he left, the nurse rushed to my side. "Are you okay? Do you need some pain meds?" She checked my brace and where it was connected to my skull. A little blood was oozing out of one of the screws. "So, that's your father, Mister Reverend," She smirked while getting some gauze and wiping away the blood.

"In all his glory," I started to sob.

"Do you need me to page Dr. Sloan, Claudia?"

"No," I was now in a full-blown sob.

"I know he hurt you. I'm going to call Dr. Lewis to get some more pain meds. Okay?"

"Okay, but please don't tell her about this, please?"

The nurse squeezed my hand and quietly walked out of the room.

CHAPTER ELEVEN

Anyone who thinks sitting in church can make you a Christian must also think that sitting in a garage can make you a car.
—Garrison Keillor

I have no objection to people's religious beliefs, but I do object to people who force their beliefs on me. My childhood was filled with religious rituals where God was meant to be feared. I knew at the age of 15 that I had strong feelings toward women. If I identified myself as a lesbian, I knew my life would be fraught with difficultly, and I would be disowned by the church. I also knew my father would find out. Our city was not that big, and news like being gay was big news. I only wished my father had disowned me and thrown me out, but instead he abused me. When I was a teenager, I prayed to God to make me straight. Day after day, I waited, but I did not change.

I did not change because I knew it was okay to be the way I was created. I do not hold any animosity against my father's God, but I always believed there were other supreme beings that watch over us. Now, I was certain thanks to Ursula and meeting the Divine Spirit.

Most people, I felt, would think I am a lesbian because of the abuse. My father is a demanding man, and because of his profession truly believes he has a direct line to God. But my father is not the reason I am gay. Sure, it did not feel good when my church shut its doors in my face. It happened, but I survived because of the divine spiritual presence that walked with me through the darkness.

I discovered this Divine Spirit on my own and with Ursula's help. Through years of attending new churches (and being thrown out), I realized that humans take The Word and interpret a meaning from it. Too often, the interpretations are wrapped around what people want to hear and not what they hear. My father is a prime example of this.

I cannot and will never condone abuse said to be done according to God's will. This is pure bullshit and an excuse for harming children and women. Simply, my Divine Spirit does not punish me for loving women. I love; therefore, I am loved. My father cannot understand that love is love. To be honest, I wonder if my father loves anyone or anything except an orgasm or multiple orgasms!

I will never understand my father and his actions, but then, I know he refuses to understand my actions. I do know that the quest for power is the driving force behind my father's actions. He wants to be in control and harming others proves to him how powerful he is. Again, pure bullshit!

"Ursula, I need you," I whispered into the dark night.

The pain meds started to work, and I could feel myself relaxing from my father's yanking on my halo brace. My neck began to loosen, and the headache that brought tears was easing. How long would I be like this? How long would it be until I would be transferred to a regular room in the hospital rather than the psych ward? How long would it take for me to return to a better life?

That is if I am meant to live a better life.

◆◆◆◆◆

I am pained to know that I am in a psych ward. As my eyes slowly roam over the completely bare room, I noticed the barred window had no curtains or blinds to warm the cool air. The room was painted liberally with hospital blue. No lamps but only overhead florescent lights that frequently made my eyes hurt. My ankles and wrists were restrained to the bed railing, and a catheter stuck out between my legs. I could not even go to the bathroom by myself. When a meal was served, the nurse would feed me like a two-year-old child. The nurses never left any silverware or dishes around, in the chance that I would try to commit suicide again.

Suicide. I thought about this word a lot. I used to think that crazy people committed suicide, but I was so wrong. I now understand how very bright people could be tortured to the brink of taking their own lives. The word should be an oxymoron since, in the act of suicide, the body hopes to end the pain rather than perpetuate the pain.

Working in the music world, I watched superstars who seemed to reach the pinnacle of success suddenly, and then drastically end their lives. From Kurt Cobain to Janis Joplin and Jim Morrison to Amy Whitehouse, drug addiction and depression were most often the smoking gun. I remember thinking, after these deaths, what a waste it was of human potential and talent. Now, I personally understand the depths of mental illness. I had no control over the family I chose, even though Ursula would disagree. I could not imagine how I would agree to be born to such a dysfunctional family. My father is a monster, and his behavior affected every member of our family.

Why I chose to attempt suicide still remains a vast mystery to me. Sure, I was super depressed over my mother's death and my father's beatings, but in my younger years I always thought I would survive my circumstances. Where did that resilience go? What happened to my fight to the finish attitude? When did the sadness go from being tolerable to unbearable? Who would have ever thought that I would be the one who ended up in a psych ward?

My sister, Judith, sure, or maybe even my younger brother Adam, but not me?

Did I miss the train by being at the airport? Did a lunar eclipse happen when I was too focused on writing song lyrics? Did those lyrics take me down a dark hole? I remember reading an article on writer, Melissa Febos, the author of *The Heart-Work: Writing About Trauma as a Subversive Act*. She was quoted as saying:

> Later that day, while serving on a panel of memoirists, I polled the audience—a room packed with a few hundred readers and writers. I asked for a show of hands: Who here has experienced an act of violence, abuse, extreme disempowerment, sexual aggression, harassment, or humiliation?
> The room fell silent as the air filled with hands.

If creative types, like writers and musicians, have issues with mental illness, then I believe there is a random defective gene in human DNA that places us at peril. Authors Sylvia Plath, Virginia Wolff, and Ernest Hemingway all chose suicide over living when they were at the very apex of the literature world. Well, I do not know their stories as well as my own, so saying they suffered from mental illness may be a stretch. But I know that mental illness is a dark secret that people do not want to talk about.

For my healing, I need to talk about mental illness. I already know I am not comfortable to openly talk about depression and anxiety, but if I want to help myself, I have to come forward. Dr. Sloan, my psychiatrist, told me that the more I talk about my suicide attempt, the more I will understand myself and why I chose this way out of life. I can feel my cheeks redden as I say this. I have lots of shame about what I did, and because I failed to get help.

"For God's sake, Claudia," I reprimanded myself, "aren't you done with the blame game?"

Tears began to fall from my eyes and I refused to hold them back. They came in a rush and all I could do was let them fall. There was no tissue box in the room, so I had to use the bed sheet to wipe away my shame.

"Wow, I must really be bad if the nurses won't even give me tissues."

As if on cue, the nurse opened the door and walked into my room.

"Hi, how are you doing?" She looked at my red face and wet eyes. "Oh, looks like I came in at a good time, huh?"

I tried to nod.

"Do you want to talk about your tears?" she prompted.

I thought about saying no, but then I remembered that I promised myself to talk about my feelings. Now was the time to start.

"Will I always feel this fragile?"

"No, no not at all. This is the part where you start healing the inside wounds as well as the outer ones. They go together."

"So there's hope for me?"

"Well, I believe in you…"

✦✦✦✦✦

"I believe in you." Is that not what the Divine Spirit said to me?

CHAPTER TWELVE

*Whatever it takes to find the real you, don't be daunted if
the rest of the world looks on in shock.*
—Stephen Richards

Several undisturbed weeks passed slowly. The rain outside my
window and the gray day made me feel morbid. Dr. Lewis told me
I had to stay in the psych ward until I was over feeling suicidal.

*How do they know? Because I do not want to eat anything or because I
keep requesting pain meds is not just cause to keep me in here. Sure, my father's
visit upset me, but he ALWAYS upsets me.*

"Hi. How are you feeling today?" a voice said from the door.
It was Emma. I tried to smile.

"Hi Em."

"You've lost weight, and you've got black circles under your
eyes," Emma said, coming closer to the side of my bed. "What's
up?"

"I want to get out of here." I pointed to my head. "And I want
this damned thing to be removed."

"I don't blame you, Claudia. You've gone through a lot." She
took my hand and held it. "Your doctor told me what Dad did to
you." Em's eyes filled with tears. "He set you back by two weeks."

I did not respond because I knew I would start sobbing.

"Claudia, you need to get well so you can put him in jail."

"What?" I couldn't believe Em's choice of words.

"You need to put Father in jail for what he's done to you and
Mom," Emma's lips quivered.

I could feel heat rise from my neck to my face.

"He's going to kill you, Claudia, I heard him say that the day after he came here."

"I'm not afraid of him anymore," I blurted out, trying to convince myself I was strong.

"I am, and I'm afraid for you." Tears filled Emma's brown eyes. "Please, Claudia, you need to have him arrested or he's going to really hurt you bad."

I saw the fear in her eyes and realized that my eyes probably had the same fear when I looked in my father's eyes.

"Listen, Em, as long as I'm in here I'm safe from him. He can't hurt me anymore." I reached for her hand.

"No," she said as she pulled her hand away from mine. "He's going to find a way to get in here and kill you. I know this because I had a dream—" she stopped herself.

"What dream?" I asked and tried to slow my breath.

"I've been having this dream," she said starting to cry, "where he comes here and kills you," Emma used her sleeve to wipe her nose.

"Em, this is a locked ward. There's no way he can get in here." I tried to convince myself.

Emma took a tissue out of her pocket and blew her nose, then took a couple of deep breaths. "He's pure evil, and he'll find a way. Will you be careful, Claudia? Please?"

"I will, Em, you know I will," I replied, knowing as Emma did that my father was devious enough to find a way into my locked psych room. Maybe I should alert Dr. Lewis and Dr. Sloan. No, I could not do that because they would think I am still crazy and keep me here longer.

I thought of the gun and wished I had it right now because I shot the wrong person.

◆◆◆◆◆

Emma returned to visit me a day later.

"I'm so sorry I upset you yesterday."

"You don't need to apologize, Em." I reached out my hand to take hers. "I believe in your dreams, and I want you to know that I did alert Dr. Lewis and Dr. Sloan. I will not allow Stanley to hurt you or me."

Emma smiled when I used my father's formal name.

"Yeah, like you can do a lot with that contraption on your head," Em pointed at my halo brace.

"Yeah, I'll gore him like an enraged buck," I laughed.

Emma smiled again. She had such a gorgeous smile.

"Well, I'm so happy to know you still have a sense of humor." Em walked to the other side of my bed and looked out the barred window. "Claudia, do you know how much Mom loved you?"

"Where did that come from?"

Em turned around and faced me. "She did, she loved you lots. And I love you, too, a lot!"

"Oh, Em," the tears streamed down my cheeks. "I've always loved you and have always wanted to protect you."

"I know that. But I didn't realize how depressed you were after Mom died. I guess I was in my own grief and didn't notice yours." Em looked down at her hands.

"Em, none of what I've done is your fault. You are not responsible. I'm the one who has to accept the blame for my actions."

"But you were hurting so badly," Em whimpered.

"And so were you." I held out my hand to her again. When she took it, I admitted, "I wasn't thinking right, but I certainly have learned a valuable lesson."

Em squeezed my hand. "Do you want to share that lesson with me?"

"Well, it's a bit bizarre."

"You know how much I love the bizarre. Tell me!" Em sat on my bed.

"Em, I met my guardian angel."

"You did, when?"

"When I was at Banning." I watched Emma's eyes closely to see if she was listening. She was. "I found out that I have a guardian bear, and she saved my life that day."

"A guardian bear?" Em wondered out loud.

"A six-foot-tall black bear with a white tuft of fur on her chest," I started, "with wings."

"Very funny, Claudia."

"I'm serious, Em. She deflected the bullet." I pointed to the scar on my forehead.

"Oh, wow." Em shook her head. "How did you find out that she was your guardian bear?"

"She told me," I stammered.

"Gee, they sure give you some strong drugs around here."

"Em, I'm serious. Ursula is her name and she brought me to a cave and helped me survive the bullet and the fall."

"You are serious," Em's eyes widened. "Were you hallucinating or dreaming?"

"At first, I thought I was hallucinating, but after a time, Ursula convinced me I was actually talking to a bear that knows seven languages including English."

"So now you speak bear, too?" Em grinned.

"Yes, I do." I winced at the realization. "Although I can't recall how to do so right now."

"Okay, so tell me what she said to you."

"She showed me past events where I saw the truth; oh, and I saw your guardian deer," I added to impress Em.

"You saw my what?" Em's eyes were wide with anticipation.

"Your guardian deer." I smiled at the memory. "She's totally white with rose-colored ears and mouth."

"You mean like an albino deer?"

"Yes," was the only answer I could muster, but suddenly added, "She's beautiful."

"Wow, imagine that an albino deer," Em closed her eyes. "I would've never guessed."

"And look," I exclaimed, showing Em the stuffed black bear she gave me.

"I never—" Em whispered. "Sis, I got that for you because I thought it was cute."

"But you intuitively knew."

Em nodded her head. "I know, I know, the gift."

"Right."

"What do you mean the bear showed you past events? I mean, how can she do that?"

"Because she's from heaven."

"Boy, you really did hit your head hard." Em wasn't smiling anymore. "What did you learn about your past?"

"A year after Ben's birth, Mom miscarried."

"She never said anything about that."

"I know she was ashamed. She miscarried me."

"And Ursula helped you see this?"

"Yeah, and as Mom was falling under the influence of the drugs they gave her, she said she loved me."

"Did she say your name?"

"Yes."

"Wow, that is so weird." Em ran her hands through her hair. "But you must have decided to be born because you're here."

"Yes. And I'm back again because Ursula showed me why I needed to return to the living."

"What did she show you?"

"She showed me that I needed to return to life because I need to face Father."

"But, I told you he wants to kill you."

"No, Em, he can't."

"Why?"

"Because Ursula and the Divine Spirit told me that Father has chosen evil over good. He needs to be put away so he can't hurt me, you, and all the others in the world."

"How are you going to get him locked up?"

"I don't know yet," I murmured.

Emma asked more and more questions, but I was so tired I had to stop our conversation. I knew Em would return to listen to more of my story.

◆ ◆ ◆ ◆ ◆

The long days turned into twelve long weeks as I still had the halo brace attached to my head. I was feeling stronger, and my neck was healing as well as Dr. Lewis expected it to.

"Good morning," a sweet voice came from a woman who appeared with a wheelchair. She was a tall, athletic-looking, black American woman with gorgeous black eyes. "I'm Nita Bernard, and I'm going to help you return to your old self." She smiled.

"Gee, I hope you have a lifetime!"

Nita laughed. "I'm a physical therapist, and I'm going to help you walk again."

"Really? I mean, the doctor is letting me move around."

"Yup, and she wants you to start today." Nita pushed the side railing down on my bed. "Now, before we help you into this chair, we need to move very slowly or you'll get dizzy."

"What makes you think I'm not already?" I replied, trying to sit up straighter. "You look familiar. Do I know you?"

"I was the drummer next to you in our high school band."

"You think? You're not sure?"

"I knew a Claudia Thomas not a Claudia Matthews."

"I changed my last name to Matthews several years ago. Wait!" My mind scrolled through my history. "Yes, yes, I remember you, Nita Bernard."

"That's me," Nita flashed a gorgeous smile.

"Wow, I remember how envious I was of your talent. Your sense of timing and rhythm were truly inspiring. I wanted to drum like you did."

"Seriously?" Nita asked, wrinkling her face.

"More than serious." I looked into her dark eyes. "I wondered what happened to you."

"Oh, I attended college and graduated with a degree in physical therapy. That's about it."

"I hope you didn't give up playing the drums. You were so good."

Nita smiled. "I played in a band for a while but was bored. I decided I wanted to help people heal."

"A noble cause," I said, suddenly embarrassed by my messy appearance. "I look like hell."

"You look great like you did back in high school." Nita slid her hands behind my back and slowly removed the pillow.

"Yeah, I remember what a sweet talker you were back then. I see you haven't changed."

"Nope, only older." Nita pushed the call button for a nurse to help her. When the other nurse came in the room, Nita said, "If you get behind Claudia, I'll position her so we can slide her over to the chair. Okay, on three, one, two, three."

I felt my body smoothly lifted off the bed and into the wheelchair. "Wow, you two are strong."

Nita and the nurse looked at each other and laughed. The nurse said, "We work out together, so we know what we're doing."

"I'm impressed," was all I could say.

Physical therapy lasted 20 minutes before I was brought back to my room.

"You look wiped," Nita said as she and the nurse put me back in bed. "Don't worry about the short time we spent together today. Our sessions will get longer as your body starts recalling how to walk."

"I look forward to that," I said, feeling somewhat uplifted.

◆◆◆◆◆

I had physical therapy on a regular basis now that I was truly feeling better. My head was still in the halo brace, but I surprised myself by getting around with it on. Infrequently I was reminded that the brace was there, like when I tried to bend down to pick up the little black bear Emma gave me when it landed on the floor.

"Hey lady, want a ride?" Nita slipped into my room with a wheelchair.

"Where are you taking me today?" I smiled, playing along with the game.

"Oh, wouldn't it be grand if we could go swim in the ocean?" she asked.

"Yeah, I can use my brace as a net to catch and cook our supper." I laughed at the thought.

"Ew, you're so domesticated." Nita replied as she held the wheelchair still for me. "But, alas, I'm sorry fair maiden because we have other surprises waiting for us." She smiled that gorgeous smile.

My heart skipped a beat.

Nita wheeled me into the physical therapy room and had me close my eyes.

"Now what are you up to?"

"Wait a minute, Claudia, I'm getting us ready."

"Oh, this should be good."

"What? You don't trust me?" I'm sure she pouted, but I couldn't see her with my eyes shut. "Okay, you can open your eyes now."

Nita sat in front of me on a chair with bongo drums between her knees.

"Well, this looks like fun," I said, enjoying the surprise.

Nita placed another set of bongo drums on my lap, and I struggled to place them between my knees.

"This is where I began my drumming." Nita placed her hands gently on the drums and started to pat the skins. A lovely sound filled the air.

I started copying her hand movements and began patting my drums. After only five minutes, I stopped exhausted.

"Tired already," Nita laughed. "Let's try a little longer."

I could not refuse her. We played the bongos like we were born with them, but then Nita progressed into her own rhapsody, and I could only sit and stare at her. A phenomenal drummer, she expertly worked her hands on the skins. The musical beat was solid, and I wanted to dance.

"What's wrong?" Nita stopped drumming.

"Will you teach me to drum like you do?"

"Absolutely, I'd be happy to." She returned her bongos to the floor and retrieved mine and set them next to hers. "Well, I think I've wiped you out for the day."

"But I loved it." I missed drumming now that I had a chance to play.

"Well, we'll graduate to the kettledrums when you get some muscles back, okay?"

"It's a deal," I replied, still smiling.

◆◆◆◆◆

My daily sessions with Dr. Sloan, my psychiatrist, and group therapy were painful in a different way than my physical therapy. The scars I had internally were not visible, but the pain was real.

"How are you doing today, Claudia?" Dr. Sloan asked. She was a small, petite, white-haired woman with a slightly crooked smile.

"I don't understand why my father chose me to be his whipping post, or why my family, except my sister Emma, have disowned me." This thought was often on my mind. "I wasn't the one who made our home life so difficult."

"It's called betrayal, Claudia." Dr. Sloan took a brief glance at her notes. "Your father and some of your siblings betrayed you."

I did not understand.

"Your mother betrayed you, too."

"No, she didn't," I responded with terror, "she's the only one who helped me."

"Claudia, you need to get in touch with the anger you have for your mother—"

"I'm not angry with her," I hotly protested.

"You should be. She could have reported your father to the police, but she didn't. She fixed your wounds, but some of your injuries needed medical attention, and she didn't take you to the emergency room." Dr. Sloan looked directly into my soul. "As your mother, she's responsible for your safety and your medical needs. She didn't take you to the doctor because she knew once the police found abuse, social services would've removed you and your siblings from home."

"No, no that's not true." My mother's image flashed through my thoughts like a knife. "I—"

"She didn't get you medical attention when you needed it. Your mother bandaged you up as best she could, but you needed some of your bones set. Her medical knowledge was minimal."

"She tried her best."

"No, if she had tried her best, she would've obtained the medical help you needed, but she didn't in order to protect herself and your father."

"That's unfair to say," I screamed.

"Unfair? No, you were treated badly and unfairly. She allowed you to be abused by your father."

"But she was protecting the family from father," tears streamed down my cheeks.

"Claudia, don't you think your mother should have protected you?"

"Well, well, my father is the evil one. My mother helped me stay alive."

"Did she?" Dr. Sloan's voice was soft and strong.

"Yes," I blurted without thinking.

"If she protected you, then why do you have so many injuries? Your x-rays show unbelievable amounts of abuse."

I stopped myself from responding. Dr. Sloan had the proof that I was beaten time after time. How could I deny the evidence of what my father did to me? And, how could I deny that my mother drove me to the doctor only on very rare occasions, then pleading with the doctor not to tell the police.

"Well, she brought me to the doctor to find out if I was pregnant," I said, slowly realizing the truth.

"She only sought medical attention when she thought you could be pregnant?"

I nodded.

"That's why you need to talk about the anger you have for your mother."

"But I trusted her with my whole soul," I cried.

"Yes, you did, because children should be protected by their mothers and fathers. There are laws to protect you."

"The laws to protect me are shit. They always were, and they always will be."

"No, Claudia, you can tell the authorities about the abuse, and they can put your father away so he doesn't abuse you, your siblings, or anyone else." Dr. Sloan leaned toward me. "Who are you protecting? Your mother?"

"She's dead."

"Yes, she is, and now you need to start protecting yourself. You need to report your father." Dr. Sloan sat back in her chair.

"But the statute of limitations is over, and I have no other option."

"When was the last time he threatened to kill you?" Dr. Sloan's eyes were so intense.

I needed to think. He threatened me after my mother's funeral saying I would be the next to die. "Maybe last year."

"Then your complaint would fall within the statute of limitations."

"But I'm in a psych ward! Who's going to believe a crazy person?"

"You're not crazy, Claudia; you were extremely abused. The x-rays are solid proof."

I froze in my hospital bed unable to move. I suddenly remembered my talk with Emma.

"No," Emma said as she pulled her hand away from mine. "He's going to find a way to get in here and kill you. I know this because I had a dream—" she stopped herself.

Emma had a dream. Yes, Emma had a dream that my father would sneak into the hospital and kill me. How had I forgotten her dream? Didn't I need to protect my life?

I looked up at Dr. Sloan. "My sister told me that my father's going to kill me.

Silence. My words hung in thick silence.

"When did your sister tell you this?"

"Last week." I lowered my eyes.

"You've known this for a week, and this is the first time you're telling me?" Dr. Sloan frowned.

I nodded.

"Claudia, this is a serious claim coming from your sister."

"I simply thought she was being overly dramatic."

"Overly dramatic? I've seen your x-rays; there's nothing overly dramatic about those. We need to protect you from him."

We need to protect you from him.

The words were the most honest words I had ever heard.

◆◆◆◆◆

BETRAYAL! Dr. Sloan had called it betrayal. I let the word swim around in my brain as my heart attempted its usual denial. I wanted so bad to believe she was wrong, but I knew she nailed it. Betrayal.

I want all of this to go away. I want to pretend this never happened. I need something to help me forget. My goal was always to flee from my father. I certainly had no intention to confront him, even though I knew what he was doing to me was evil. But I doubted I had the case to send him to jail.

"Why not?" I asked myself knowing I tried everything to avoid feeling hurt. In my effort to make the pain go away, I tried suicide. I did not succeed, and now I am in a psych ward too fragile to return to the real world.

I searched my room seeing nothing but blue walls, my hospital bed, a window with bars on it, and the small stuffed bear Emma gave me. That was all my life consisted of at the moment. Didn't I deserve more from life?

I want to return to my apartment and sleep in my own bed. I want to see my friends and to laugh again. I want to get back to my writing and create new songs, songs of triumph and victory.

Betrayal. Damn, I did not want to write songs about betrayal.

"You took my heart that day, with all its joy, and now you walk the other way..." The familiar lyric flashed across my thoughts, making me realize that I had already written about betrayal. I did not remember it that way.

Betrayal, right in my face betrayal! It was always there, but I did not want to see it. And now, Dr. Sloan brought the dream to the surface and I could no longer ignore the truth.

My father betrayed me by beating me and making me feel dirty. He betrayed my love with hate and my sense of belonging with being alone. Some of my siblings betrayed me by disowning me, by keeping me isolated from the family that should love and respect me. They betrayed me by refusing to see my injuries and my cry for help. They betrayed me by saying that I was responsible for the consequences of my beatings, that I deserved the treatment I got from my father. Except for Emma, they all betrayed me because they did not want to see the reality of what our family is: sick!

My ancestors knew we were all sick, and they wanted us to heal. They could not do it, and now it was in my hands. Shit, why me?

I was not the strongest or the most intelligent, but I always knew I would survive even the worst beatings. Now I had the chance to heal myself and, maybe, even my ancestors.

And though I hated to admit it, the truth was my mother betrayed me, too. This was the greatest betrayal of all.

"The greater the trust that you put in another person, the greater the impact their betrayal has on you, and the greater the distress you feel," Dr. Sloan had said. "A number of different emotions are felt when you realize you've been betrayed. The most common is anger. You fear the loss of the relationship with your mother, but are repulsed by her lack of integrity."

Dr. Sloan was right, of course, but the most unnerving thing I had to deal with was when she said, "From a personal view, justice means making you feel better. From a community view, it means carrying out the law, regardless of how frightening this may seem."

My father is a criminal, actively participating in unlawful behavior. He raped me and physically hurt me with torture. He's a narcissistic sociopath who believes he is doing God's work.

"Bullshit," I said aloud, "bullshit." I could not grasp how my father could feel he was doing good work, yet I know that he had always been an expert illusionist.

"Why don't other people see what he's doing?" I asked myself. "Because his actions are so horrific, and most of the time people can't fathom the amount of evil he spreads. Their denial, along with some of my siblings, is something I don't understand and never will."

I wondered how my mother married such an evil man. Mom was beautiful with long brunette hair, a perfect smile (until my father knocked out her two front teeth) and large gray eyes. Her fingers were thin and dainty looking, but she often kept her scarred hands in her pockets. Mom was an only child, which made her fiercely proud of her children. She would never let the people in town know that she was being beaten by her husband.

"Why Mom, why did you stay with him?" I pondered. "I'll never love someone like him," I promised that to myself all this time.

I had a few relationships in the past, but none ever lasted more than six months. I did not trust love and when my feelings began to deepen, I moved on. Love to me was being tied down to someone who had as much emotional garbage as I did. That thought alone made me very leery about being in a long relationship. I wondered if my mother thought she did not deserve better than my father. Hmmm, I bet that's what she believed.

I closed my eyes. Was that my fear, too? Yes, I did not believe I would ever find a partner who was emotionally healthy.

"There's someone for everyone," Ursula had said. *"Someone who will love you and never betray you."*

I forgot she said this when we talked about relationships.

"What makes a good relationship?" I remember asking Ursula.

"A good relationship includes love, trust, respect, and honesty." She placed her paw on her heart. I could feel the intense heat from her fur. "Healthy relationships have their ups and downs, but the downs never last. Talking openly is vitally important in creating great relationships. You have to be willing to open up yourself and reveal where you're most vulnerable."

"Yikes, Ursula, that sounds like a disaster to me."

"No, opening up lays the foundation in every relationship. For it to be a solid foundation both of you have to reveal your vulnerabilities."

"Sounds like a recipe for disaster."

"Not necessarily, because you also share your strengths. Two closed hearts cannot forge a lasting relationship. Neither can a relationship succeed if only one heart is open." Ursula paused, "Have you ever had a conversation with a wall?"

"A wall? No, never."

"Why not?"

"Because walls don't talk."

"My point exactly," Ursula smiled. "If only one person in a relationship is talking, then it is not a conversation. Conversations between two people are necessary for growth."

I thought about Ursula's words.

"You and I converse and, in return, you feel safe to ask me questions, right?" Ursula's question was more like a statement.

"Yeah, but I still have problems getting used to talking to a black bear."

"A very special black bear, I might add." Ursula winked.

Do bears wink, I asked myself. "Okay, if I want to have a good relationship with direct communication, how do I begin?"

"By asking questions of others like you have asked me."

"It's that simple?" I shook my head. "Asking questions?"

Ursula raised her paws to the sun. "Yes, that's it exactly!"

"Sounds so simple."

"It is. There's no better way to get to know people than by asking them questions. Honest questions, I might add. You have to be sure your questions don't throw people off. A lot of questions can be very personal, which makes people defensive."

"What if I ask a question and the person says to me 'it's none of your business'?"

"Well, it could mean that you asked a very personal question or the person was not open to talking with you. So bam! End of conversation."

"And that would be an example of one heart open and one heart closed."

"Exactly!" Ursula sat on her haunches. "Humans often start conversations with comments about the weather. 'Boy, it sure is a hot one today, isn't it?' And the reply is 'Yeah, I'm hoping for rain soon.'"

"And that's an example of two open hearts?"

"Right, in its simplest form of communication."

"So I should never go up to a stranger and ask, 'What's been your worst nightmare?'"

Ursula laughed, at least that is what it sounded like.

I had to laugh, too. It was a really dumb question. I suddenly felt like I wanted to hug Ursula.

◆◆◆◆◆

"There's someone for everyone."

CHAPTER THIRTEEN

*You must learn a new way to think
before you can master a new way to be.*
—Marianne Williamson

The weather outside my hospital window was stormy with rain pouring down and lightning flashing all around. I love storms because of the energy that is released into the atmosphere and the pure cleansing of the air. Storms always make me feel that I can restart my life all over again, and today that was my goal.

"Good morning, Claudia," Nita said as she steered the wheelchair to my bedside. "Are you ready to tackle the machines today?"

"Yup, and I want to walk today,"

"Wow! I love your attitude." Nita started to remove the sheets off my legs.

"Wait, let me do this," I said as I pushed the sheets off my legs and hung them over the side of the bed. I rose up on shaking legs and quickly lowered my body into the chair.

"Very impressive!" Nita smiled again as she released the wheelchair's brakes.

It did not take us long to arrive at the physical therapy area. I rolled my wheelchair to the end of the parallel bars.

"What are you up to, Ms. Claudia?"

"The brace is gone and I've decided that I want to walk today."

"Are you sure? I mean that's a big step for you," Nita cautioned as she tilted her head to the side while watching my face.

"Today's the day!" I could feel my smile spread from ear to ear. "The halo brace was removed two days ago and there's nothing holding me back."

"Okay, boss, let me get into position." Nita walked between the bars and stopped in front of me. "Place your hands on the bar, and I'll help you stand up."

Lightning flashed outside the window as a loud clap of thunder filled the room.

"This storm is growing fierce," Nita observed. "I love storms."

"Me, too," I replied, slowly moving my head from right to left and back again. "I love the energy in the air from the lightning."

Nita nodded. "And the clean air that follows."

Lightning flashed again and the lights flickered.

"Hmm, maybe we should wait for the storm to pass," Nita said.

"No, today is the day I walk."

"You're sure?" Nita cautioned.

I nodded. "It's now or never!"

Nita helped me stand and guided my hands onto the bars. My legs began to shake, and I felt light-headed. When another bolt of lightning flashed thunder quickly followed. Nita looked out the window, saying, "I think Mother Nature is angry with us."

"Yeah, but it's giving me the energy to try to walk." We were standing face to face.

"Okay, I want you to slowly put one foot in front of the other, okay?"

I did as I was instructed, and my legs tried to follow, but they were still very weak. My legs began to shake more.

"Oh, crap, don't give up on me now legs," I encouraged my body.

"You're doing really good, Claudia, please go slow."

I attempted another step and then another. I was feeling really pumped after the first five steps.

"Okay, let's turn around and go back to your chair."

"I'm actually walking," my enthusiasm was growing. When I got back to the wheelchair, I resisted sitting down. "I can't stop now," I said, feeling the storm's energy rushing through my veins. I turned and faced Nita and stepped forward as lightning and thunder arrived simultaneously. I jumped in surprise and fell into Nita's arms.

The lights in the room went out.

I could feel Nita's arms around me. The physical contact surprised me. She was so strong and I could feel her muscles underneath my arms.

Something in my heart cracked open.

The lights came back on.

"Well, well, it looks like the storm has turned on the black and white lezzies," a voice said from the doorway. My father used a derogative term for lesbians.

I tried to look, but my neck was a bit too stiff to turn that far to the right. But I knew that voice. I began to shake.

"You're not allowed in here," Nita asked looking over my shoulder. "Who are you?"

"I'm her father," he said as he walked toward the parallel bars.

I cursed under my breath, but Nita heard my dismay. She backed me up and lowered me on to the wheelchair.

"Like I said, you're not allowed in here." Nita glanced quickly at me and then back to my father. I'm sure my face was pale.

"I wanted to see how she's doing in her recovery," my father touched one of the bars. "I didn't realize she's already reached the groping stage."

"Look, Mister…"

"That's Reverend to you."

"Look, Mister Reverend, I want you to turn around and walk out that door before I call security."

I knew Nita could feel me shaking. She squeezed my hand and pushed the wheelchair back so she could get in my father's face. In fact, she stood face to face with him as she was the same height.

With her hand Nita pushed my father back toward the door. "Get out."

"You can't tell me what to do, you little lezzie," he sneered.

With that, Nita seized him by the arm and escorted him to the door and pushed the security button. I could hear footsteps racing down the hall. Two uniformed security guards rushed through the door.

"I don't know how he got in here, but I want him out now!" Nita pushed my father toward the security guards. "Make sure he never drops in on me and my patient again," she snarled.

With my back to all the commotion, I could sense my father's anger rising past the danger level.

"Dammit!" Nita yelled as the two security guards pulled my father's arm away from Nita's face and forced him down the hall.

When Nita came back to me her nose was bleeding.

"Nita! Nita! He punched you?"

"Oh, it was only a poke, nothing to worry about." Nita grabbed some tissue from a box and held it to her nose.

"I'm so, so sorry! I have no idea how he breached security. Does your nose hurt?" I reached out my shaking hands.

Nita held one of my hands and squeezed. "Like I said, it was only a poke." Her eyes turned as dark as the sky outside.

"I'm really sorry," I gulped.

"Let's get you back to your room," Nita said abruptly as she wheeled me out of the room.

◆◆◆◆◆

That afternoon during her daily visit, Dr. Lewis, my primary doctor, examined my head.

"It looks like your neck is doing okay since we removed your brace, Claudia."

"How long did I have it on?"

Dr. Lewis looked at her notes. "Well, we had to tack on an extra week when your father pulled your brace, but it now seems that nine weeks has been good for your head and neck. They've healed well." The doctor lowered my chart. "Speaking of your father, Claudia —"

"Oh, I'm so very sorry about what happened this morning to Nita," I felt mortally embarrassed.

"Your father broke Nita's nose this morning, and we're pressing assault charges against him."

"He broke her nose?" I gasped.

"Yes. She's doing fine, but we need to protect our employees. We've tightened security."

"How did he get in?"

"During the storm, when the lights went out, and while we switched to an emergency generator, the locks were all compromised. He was able to walk right in." Dr. Lewis looked out the window.

"I'm so sorry," I said again.

"I know you are, but we can't have this happen again."

Dr. Lewis turned her eyes away from the window and looked at me. "Claudia, we want you to file assault charges against your father, too."

I couldn't look at Dr. Lewis because my shame was so deep. Instead I closed my eyes. Today was the day to start again.

"Yes," I said softly, "he needs to be stopped."

CHAPTER FOURTEEN

Courage is being afraid but going on anyhow.
—Dan Rather

After three months blurred by, I was comfortably sitting at my desk in my apartment feeling alone. The bookshelves, filled with my favorite novels and picture frames, reflected my love of nature. But, even sitting in my old pair of jeans and wearing my favorite long-sleeved t-shirt could not raise my mood.

I was released from the hospital two weeks ago when I had the courage to get a restraining order, so my father could not attack me. I still walk with a cane. I feel physically better, but my present state of mind is troubled.

In the past two months, I had not seen Nita at all. Another physical therapist was assigned to me after my father broke Nita's nose. I tried to contact her, but my requests were not answered. After months and months of physical therapy, I enjoyed Nita and her marvelous sense of humor. She was a woman who stood up for her beliefs and was always helping others. Her absence in my life made my loneliness feel even deeper.

And she was so beautifully honest. That is why I could not figure out why she left. I thought I would at least get a note from her saying she couldn't be my physical therapist after my father hurt her. But her silence was disturbing. Most likely I blew up my importance to her thinking I was special when I really was but another patient. Yet, there were those moments when I fell into her arms the day my father showed up.

Too many pain killers.

Once I was off all pain medications, the cold hard truth was more than I could bear. I was alone, except for Emma's visits.

Here it was, 12:30 a.m. and I could not sleep, could not write, and could not raise my own spirits. With my head in my hands, I again thought about suicide.

"STOP IT!" I yelled as I arose from my chair. "JUST STOP IT!" I stood still for a moment and breathed deeply. Dr. Sloan, my psychiatrist, had taught me how to catch myself from being depressed by deep breathing. I inhaled a deep breath of air, counted to four, and then slowly exhaled. I did this four times before I gathered my wits. My pulse returned to normal, and I felt calm course through my body.

The large oak, pendulum clock on the wall ticked out my loneliness and despair. The silence in the room was heavy, and I could feel my heart begin to race. I believed life would be different after my suicide attempt, but nothing seemed to have changed. I returned to work and spent time with friends, but my future seemed so empty.

I walked to the window and peered out on the street. No people were on the street and all seemed quiet. The full moon reflected off the parked cars, including my SUV. When I was found at Banning the police called Emma to pick up my car in the pound lot. She'd been using it while I was in the hospital.

Emma. Beautiful full-of-life Emma. She was my best friend and checked on me daily. When I returned home to my apartment from the hospital, a huge bouquet of colorful flowers greeted my return. Emma was sunshine on a dreary gray day. With her permission, I added her name to the restraining order I filed on my father. I did not want him to hurt her. Out of five children in our family, she was the only one to stand by my side. Judith, Adam, and Ben were no-shows in my life. This confused me because I never hurt them or caused them to be in trouble with my father.

Dr. Sloan had explained to me that incredible as it might seem, some families scapegoat a loved one even into and including adulthood. I became the target of accusations, blame, criticism, and ostracism, all the while knowing my siblings were unaware of what they were doing. I knew they would deny it if I confronted them with their behavior. My father's influence of scapegoating me, unfortunately, began in my childhood and continues with my siblings.

When I asked Dr. Sloan why a family would choose a loved one to bully and scapegoat, she informed me it has a lot to do with the concept of scapegoating and the purpose it serves.

"Scapegoating is often a way for dysfunctional families like yours to hide problems they can't face. In adulthood, and in your family dynamics, scapegoating becomes a way for your siblings to hide the family history of abuse by blaming the one member who seemed vulnerable for attack."

"I don't think I was looked on as being vulnerable."

"But you were often being taken care of by your mother." Dr. Sloan stated. "They may have viewed this as the reason you are seen as the most favored sibling, and that is why you become the source of dysfunction in your family."

"But we're adults now. Can't they see that I didn't cause the problems in the family?"

"While you'd think this should not be a problem for an adult, the fact is that you became depressed, anxious, withdrawn, and even suicidal. There is no way to underestimate the fears, self-hatred, and desperation you feel. It's so common for you to believe what the family tells you, so you accept all of the blame and pointing fingers, even though it's untrue."

"So, I am nuts after all?"

"No, no far from it." Dr. Sloan smiled. "In fact, you're probably the most normal person in your family."

"Can you tell that to them?"

"Sure, but there's years of lies and untruths in your family."

"So, they wouldn't believe you?"

"It would be very painful for all of them to accept that your father is the perpetrator," Dr. Sloan pronounced.

"Really?" Dr. Sloan's answer blew my mind. I couldn't believe my siblings would choose to disbelieve me and see my father as a hero.

"Yes, I'm afraid so."

"So, do I write them out of my life, I mean, except for Emma?"

"Well, Claudia, I always say there occurs a moment of truth when the lies can no longer be hidden. They have to see the damage your father did and come to understand he betrayed them, too."

"I've been waiting for that moment of truth for years."

Dr. Sloan nodded and added, "Keep believing in the truth. You didn't ask your father to hurt you. He singled you out and was abusive. Your siblings may not want to believe he's so evil. It could be frightening for them."

"It was frightening for me!"

"Absolutely, and that's why we need to free you from the scapegoat label."

◆◆◆◆◆

After 3 a.m., I am finally in bed thinking over the conversation I had with Dr. Sloan. I believe she is a very wise woman. Ursula would like her, I thought. I smiled.

"Ursula," I whispered in the dark room, "I miss you so much. Help me do what's right for the right reasons. I'm sorry I considered suicide tonight, but it was a moment of hopelessness. I was letting fear make me weak."

I closed my eyes and finally surrendered to sleep.

◆◆◆◆◆

When I opened my eyes the next morning, I was filled with frightening confusion. Was my father really standing at the end of my bed with a large knife? I shook my blurry head. The bedroom was filled with early morning light and the recent paint on the walls was a mellow blue. Nightmares could seem so real.

Emma ran into my room screaming, "Claudia, he's going to kill you! Get up!"

I scrambled to my feet on the bed and hung on to a pillow. "Em, call the police," I shouted.

"Make that call and I'll kill you both," my father taunted, his eyes red and wild with hatred. He walked to the doorway and blocked it with his big girth, trapping Em and me in the room.

"You won't get away with this, STAN," I said, using his proper name. I knew this would enrage him as he swayed. It had worked in the past. "You're past drunk and smell like a bar. Why don't you go home and make yourself some coffee?"

"I-don't-need-coffee," he slurred. He was trying hard to keep his eyes focused on me.

"Why are you doing this?" I stepped toward him. I was terrified he was going to hurt Emma, but I was not afraid he was going to hurt me. The time had arrived to stand up to my father, if not for me then for Emma. "You've done enough harm to our family. I won't let you do more." I inhaled a deep breath. "You're already in trouble with the police."

"I can do what I want with my children," he pointed the knife at Emma. "I am all powerful."

"No!" I took another step toward him. "No, you're a sorry excuse for a man, STAN." I edged to the end of the bed. He looked at Em and then at me. When he realized how close I was to him, he smiled.

"Yes, Claudia, save your sister—"

I jumped off the bed and charged him with the pillow. I saw the knife blade come through the pillow as I attacked. He couldn't stand against me because of the force I created and the beer he had consumed. He fell backward landing on his back.

"Run, Em, run!" She flew by me.

My father tried to retrieve his knife out of the pillow. "I'm gonna kill you, bitch!"

When I met Emma at the front door, we opened it, me in my pajamas and Em in her jogging suit, and raced outside. We arrived at the corner store and called 911.

By the time the police searched my apartment, my father had vanished. My pillow lay on the floor in shreds. A police photographer appeared and started taking pictures of the scene. One cop walked Emma to the kitchen to record her story as I sat on the couch with another cop.

"Tell me what happened," he asked.

I explained to him everything I could remember that morning, but it all seemed like a bad nightmare. My hands were shaking, and the police officer placed a blanket over my shoulders.

"You need to change your locks today and get a security system," he instructed. "We've put out a warrant on your father and will arrest him."

"We had a restraining order on him," I said, feeling so tired.

"That's why we're going to arrest him." He stood up as the other cop appeared from the kitchen with Emma. I walked them to the door and showed them out. I leaned back on the door after I closed it. I closed my eyes. "How did you know he was here?"

"I couldn't sleep last night, so I dressed and walked around the neighborhood. You know how I know when something bad is going to happen, so I walked over to your place to see if you were up yet. I saw him slide something like a credit card through your lock. Your door opened."

"I didn't even hear anything." I shook my head.

Emma walked into my bedroom with the small black bear she had given me in the hospital. "Here," she said, handing it to me, "I know you need your guardian bear."

◆◆◆◆◆

I held the stuffed black bear in my arms as I tried to recover from this latest assault.

CHAPTER FIFTEEN

*The day you stop blaming others is the day
you begin to discover who you truly are.*
—Anonymous

My father's photo was splashed across the next day's newspaper
with the headline, "Local Minister Arrested Trying to Kill His
Children." Emma informed me the congregation at my father's
church were stunned, and many members were in total disbelief.
Some even believed that the charges were made up to punish this
man of God.

However, others believed that the charges were real and knew
my father was a control freak. His anger was not always so easy to
hide as my mother tried so valiantly to do. People saw through him
and denounced his evil acts. He was stripped of his duties at the
church and spent the next several days in jail.

I was informed by the police department that my father would
be tried for assault, battery, and an intent to kill Emma and me.
When I discovered I would have to testify, the thought made me
sick.

My apartment procured a new security system, and the mess
my father caused was cleaned up by friends who rallied to my side.
Picking up the pillow feathers in my bedroom, my friend Denise
was sad. I sat on the bed with her.

"Claudia, why didn't you ever tell me about your father and
what he's done to you? I would've protected you with my life," big
tears appeared in Denise's green eyes.

"I was too ashamed," I said meekly.

"But he hurt you so bad. We've been friends since childhood and, though I had my suspicions, I never wanted to embarrass you. I wish I had had the courage to ask you what was going on."

"Denise, my father was horrible, but I tried to minimize how much the neighborhood knew what he was really like."

"You're not the only family in the city who has a mean and abusive father. My father used to kick me around until I held a knife to his throat." Denise's words were haunting.

"When did you do that?" I was filled with admiration.

"When I was 12."

"Did he stop?"

"Yeah, and then I told my mom for added protection." Denise rose up from the bed and moved to the window. "My parents divorced soon after. He never hurt me again, but he didn't like me very much."

"Who cares? He hurt you." I said incredulously.

"I know, but I was only 12 years old, too little to understand the magnitude of what could've happened. And then I hear your story, and I'm glad my father doesn't like or love me."

"Do you ever see him?"

"Absolutely not. He doesn't deserve to be called my father."

"Wow, I wish I'd been as strong as you, Denise." I hung my shoulders.

Denise returned back to the bed. "I always knew you and I had a special bond, but I never questioned it. I wish you would've told me the truth."

Tears splashed down my cheeks, and I could feel my heart pounding against my rib cage. "I'm so sorry. I was too afraid to let anyone in."

"I totally understand that, but it doesn't make it right." Denise squeezed my hand.

"No, it doesn't. Had I confided in you maybe things would have been different."

"Or not," Denise said with a sigh. "We have no idea how it would've turned out. I'm so grateful that you're alive and getting the help you need."

"Thanks, Denise. I hope I can repair my friendships."

"You can by not being such a mystery!" Denise laughed. She hit me in the shoulder and stood up looking around the room. There was no trace that my father had been here.

"I love this apartment, and I don't intend to move. It's been the only home I've ever known because I was the one who created this space, this home. He wouldn't force me out on my own home." I stated with resolve.

"Right on, girlfriend." Denise walked toward the door. "I've got to run, but if you need anything, you've got my number." She smiled and left my apartment.

The relief I felt that the abuse was finally over was a blessing. And so were my friends, who didn't understand, but were by my side over the years. But I was also angry, and those feelings that had been pent up inside me for so many years threatened to appear. So, I decided that the best way I could deal with the anger was to be physically active. I purchased a rowing machine after I was released from the hospital. Every time I felt tension or unease, I would get on the rowing machine and work out. I played soothing music while I worked out so I could rest my mind and mend my heart.

◆◆◆◆◆

When I was on the rowing machine, I heard a knock on the door. I pushed back from the machine, stood, and peered through the peek hole. Thinking it was Denise, I was astonished to see my sister, Judith. I slowly opened the door.

"Hi, can I come in?" she asked, her body shaking.

I opened the door wider and gestured for her to come in.

"I know you're surprised to see me."

"I am."

She wore a black coat and her purse and shoes matched, like always. She looked like she was going to a funeral. I could see her hands trembling.

"Do you want some tea or coffee?"

"Do you have something stronger?"

I raised my eyebrows at her suggestion. Judith never drank.

"I've got some red wine."

"That'd be great," she sighed.

I retrieved two glasses of wine and returned to the living room to find her sitting on the couch. Before I could ask her why she had come she blurted out, "I'm sorry, Claudia, I'm so very sorry for taking Dad's side. I had no idea he hurt you so badly."

"How can you say that? You saw my bruises and broken bones; how can you say you had no idea?"

Judith looked down at her hands. She sipped her wine. "I looked away. I, I didn't want to believe he was so disturbed."

I found it difficult to comfort her even though I could see the now-distinct wrinkles around her gray eyes and the pallor of her skin. She was always so tan and her facial features nearly perfect. Now she was white as a ghost.

"I don't know what to tell you," I offered after a minute of heavy silence.

"I know," she answered, and for the first time looked me in the eyes. "I know, I was wrong to say you were the reasons for the tension in our family." She raised the glass of wine to her lips when her sleeve slipped back.

I could see the bloody gauze bandages wrapped around her left wrist. I quickly arose from my chair next to the couch and sat beside her. I held her arm and examined her wrist.

"Judith, you cut your wrist!" I exclaimed with bile rising in my throat.

She nodded. "I can't live knowing all this," she sobbed.

"I completely understand."

Judith glanced at her wrist with no emotion. "I thought he was a good man. Did he, did he really have sex with you?"

I nodded. "Yes, yes, many times."

"Is that why you're a lesbian?" Her eyes grew wide.

"It's not the reason, but it didn't help me emotionally or physically," I answered truthfully. "I was born this way and I'm not afraid to say it."

Blood began to drip from the gauze and formed a puddle on her coat.

"Judith, Judith how much did you cut your wrist?" I scolded as I flew out of the room to get a wet towel.

She was crying when I returned to the couch. I unwound her bandage and could see the deep slit.

"It's only my left wrist," she said, her voice filled with troubled remorse.

"Judith, you're really hurt. I'm calling 911. Okay?"

She nodded, but her head drooped. She looked dead.

When the paramedics arrived, I rode with Judith in the ambulance. All the while she was at my house, she was losing blood. Her black coat hid much of the blood, but now I knew how badly she hurt herself.

My psychiatrist Dr. Sloan had been right. Everyone in our family had been hurt by my father, but they showed it in different ways. Judith's frigid reaction to me was her way of coping. Our father's deeds had affected Judith deeply. I was shocked to realize this since I always felt she was immune to my suffering.

I had terribly misjudged Judith.

◆◆◆◆◆

All I could do was watch the medics attend to her cut wrist. When she was placed on oxygen, the color finally started to reappear on her pale cheeks. She continued to mumble in a nondescript fashion. I could hear her repeatedly crying out, "I'm so sorry." A male doctor with a military haircut and black-framed glasses appeared and instructed the nurse to add morphine to ease Judith's discomfort. I departed the room and walked down the hallway.

I leaned hard against the wall, trying to stop myself from running out of the hospital.

Judith, poor Judith. I knew I needed to open up my heart to her and my brothers Adam and Ben. This was going to be difficult, but it was a resolution I had to make.

◆◆◆◆◆

I sat in the family lounge in the hospital. After the paramedics brought Judith to the emergency room and the medical staff stitched her up, she was admitted to the psych ward. The walls and floors in the hospital looked the same when I was released nearly two and a half weeks ago. Time trickled by as if the present moment were in slow-motion. Five hours passed since I arrived at the hospital with Judith.

"Hi," Emma walked in and sat beside me. She laid her hand on my thigh and squeezed it. "How are you?"

"Better than Judith."

"I'm not surprised she hurt herself," Emma whispered. "I watched her sliding down for months, but she wouldn't let me help her."

"But you were there for her, and she knew it."

Emma nodded.

"Imagine her degree of denial. I mean, she's spent years trying to hide the truth. Her defense system overloaded." I added.

"How long do you think they'll keep her?"

"Not as long as me," I said with a grimace. "She'll have to confront a lot of ugly truths and deal with the fact that she did nothing to help Mom or us. When your make-believe-world blows up in your face, you need a lot of time to readjust to reality."

Em nodded. "I hope she can."

"She will." I caught Em's hand. "She's a survivor like you and me. She needs to know that she doesn't have to go through this alone." I released Em's hand and stood. I need some coffee. Do you want anything?"

"No thanks, I wanted to see Judith, but it looks like today isn't possible."

"Yeah, they've got her on morphine. I wanted to be here for her when she wakes up."

"You're a good sister, Claudia. I want you to know that I love you, and I'm so grateful we're facing this together. I don't know what I'd do without you."

Em gave me a hug. The human contact was beyond mere comfort. Her hair smelled of citrus, and the texture felt like cashmere. I loved my younger sister with all my heart because she was both gentle and fierce. Her smoky brown eyes gave her an air of worldliness. Emma's dreams were prophetic and as she grew to embrace this ancestral gift, she was learning how to put these dreams to foster good. I really believe that my father was afraid of Emma and her mystic nature.

We walked to the elevators.

"Keep her in your heart, Em. It's going to be a long road for her."

"I know; we all need to accept the truth. I didn't think that Dad affected Judith, but I was wrong. She saws things, too, but refused to do anything to help. Of course, I have to look at the fact that I never helped either. I'm as guilty as Judith, Ben, and Adam." Emma said as the elevator door closed.

◆◆◆◆◆

I moved along the line at the cafeteria with my tall Styrofoam cup of coffee. It was my fourth cup today, but thankfully I only drank decaf. I wondered if my breath reeked like a coffee bean container. After I paid for the coffee, I started walking down the hall.

"Oh, I'm so sorry, please excuse—" a tall woman said as she turned to face me.

"No prob—" I started to say.

"Claudia!" the woman said, her deep brown eyes wide.

"Nita, it's been a long time," I replied as my heart raced. Seeing Nita for the first time in eight weeks was uncomfortable.

"What are you doing in the hospital?" she asked and then, "Are you here for an appointment?"

"No, my sister was admitted to the psych ward."

"What happened?" Her eyes peered intensely at me.

"My father's been arrested," I suddenly felt exhausted.

"I saw it in the newspaper. Are you okay?"

I nodded. "The truth almost destroyed my sister," I gestured toward the psych ward.

"Your father—"

I closed my eyes. There was so much I wanted to say to Nita, but I couldn't find the words.

"Can you talk?" Nita asked. "We can talk in the lounge if you like."

Again, I nodded. She led me to the lounge at the end of the hall. Luckily, the room was empty.

"I need to apologize," Nita said as we sat down on the couch.

"For what?" My mind raced. "I need to apologize to you. I didn't know my father broke your nose."

"Oh, you heard about that," she wrung her hands. Her long black hair hung behind her in a braid. Her eyes were the same intense brown. She raised her hand to her nose and let her index finger touch it.

"Does it still hurt, Nita?"

"No, I was just remembering that day." She stood and walked away from the couch. "I've been called to testify against your father."

I nodded but remained silent. Dressed in navy hospital scrubs Nita was as beautiful as the last time I saw her. I shook my head trying to dislodge the physical contact between us when I fell into her arms during physical therapy. Actually, since I was now telling the truth, that was the day I realized I was in love with her. I smiled to myself.

"It's all over the media. No escaping this if I tried." I couldn't escape the image of Nita's bloody nose. I shook my head again and lowered my eyes. "I've been asked to testify, too."

"Claudia, you've been through a lifetime of pain so far, but you're here watching over your sister. That takes courage and strength." Nita lowered her eyes to her hand. "You're amazing."

It was weird to see Nita this self-conscious. Usually she was telling a joke or encouraging me to walk farther in physical therapy. I never imagined she'd be shy.

"Do you want to know why I let someone else take over your physical therapy?" Nita began pacing.

"Well, my shit-for-a-father broke your nose."

Nita stopped looked at the floor. "It wasn't the broken nose."

"It's because I'm such a crazy person."

"Claudia, I never thought you were crazy. You had good reason to want to end all the abuse. You cried out for help and obtained medical help."

"Yeah, but I certainly made a mess with my suicide attempt."

"I don't see it that way. All the abuse and violence you dealt with amazes me. I mean, I mean I don't know many people who could carry on like you did for so long." She returned to the couch.

"You make me sound like a superhero."

"But you are!" Nita sat up and placed my hands in hers. "You are Wonder Woman, and, through your struggle I had a front-row seat to watch you regain your stamina and fight the fight."

For some reason, I found it comforting to hold hands with Nita. Her long thin fingers wrapped around my hands like a soft blanket. In the past, I would've yanked my hands away from such intimacy.

"Claudia, I left because—" Nita stopped herself.

"Because—" I prompted.

"Because I was falling in love with you."

Her statement hung in the air for several minutes.

"Oh?" I said, suddenly feeling giddy.

"Yes." Nita moved my bangs away from my eyes. "I ran because I was a member of your medical team and I shouldn't have had those feelings for you. It's not professionally correct."

"Hmmm, professionally correct?" I said, trying to buy some time to think about my response.

"But I can't stop thinking about you," Nita softly said.

"I wish we were a year away from now." I examined my hands. "I'm going to testify at my father's trial, and I need to focus. If I tell you that I love you, too, I'm afraid we'll run off and get lost in the moment. I can't do that right now. I can't do that to us. I'm sorry, Nita."

Nita's eyes filled with tears. "I've never been rejected so kindly."

"I'm not rejecting you," I stammered. "I do need to end my father's rule over me so I can live my own life. I want freedom and love."

"I understand, Claudia, but I also want you to know that I'm here for you when we take on your father. You need protection, I'll protect you! You need support, I'm here. You need a shoulder to cry on, I'm here!"

Tears rolled down my cheeks, and I tried to speak but choked on my sobs.

"I'll wait for you, Claudia." Nita stood and picked up her long gray coat, black-brimmed gray hat, and leather gloves. She put on the outdoor clothes and exited the lounge.

The familiar sight of the long gray coat, black-brimmed gray hat, and black leather gloves stopped me. My heart raced as I remembered the unknown woman standing over my cemetery marker. She was wearing these exact items.

"It was Nita," I whispered and began to cry.

◆◆◆◆◆

I rested at my regular coffee shop, thinking about my conversation with Nita. I admit I have feelings for her, very strong feelings, and I know it would end in disaster if I should act on them now. There is so much going on in my life with my father and my siblings that I wonder if I have the energy for a relationship.

"I'll wait for you," Nita's words slid slowly lingering in my mind.

My coffee shop is in a small northern suburb with a pretty good customer base. I like it here because the coffee's good and I can sit by the window and lose myself in my own world. People arrive and depart, but I am not bothered, or maybe I am giving off nonverbal signals that I choose to be left alone. Today's cup of decaf coffee is particularly delicious. As I swallow another mouthful, the warm liquid glides down my throat. I have a few obsessions, but I do love my cup of coffee each morning. It helps me enter the day with a spiritual comfort, sort of what religion does for others.

When I look out the large window with lace curtains, I notice a woman I had not seen before entering the coffee shop. She comes in, orders some tea and sits at the table next to mine. Her skin is the color of the brown Earth, and her long gray hair is braided and cascades down her back to her hips. The handmade jewelry she wears is a brilliant contrast to her blouse and skirt. She smiles at me as she sets her tea on the table and sits down. I return to looking out the window thinking about my father's future if there even is one.

My father. He finally was caught and is in jail for assault and attempted murder. Em and I met with a lawyer to ensure our safety. The lawyer, Mary Beth Hart, a friend from college, practiced domestic violence cases. Father was going to be tried, and we would be called as witnesses. Mary Beth told us that telling the truth was our most important objective. She encouraged me to write down what my father had done to me and not to soften the abuse.

"Tell the truth Claudia and the jury will side with you."

"*The truth*," I typed on my laptop. Emma had talked about the truth. But how does one take years of abuse and pain and whittle it down to a succinct story? A succinct believable story? I swallowed more coffee and rested my head in my hands. "I can't do this," I whimpered to myself.

"Start with the basics," said an unfamiliar voice. "You know how to write, and you know how to present your story." I shook my head because I had no idea where to begin.

"Start at the beginning," the voice said.

I raised my head from my hands and peered directly at the stranger sitting at the next table. Her eyes were so dark brown that they appeared black. When I smiled, she smiled back.

"I'm sorry. I didn't mean to interrupt your thoughts," the woman said, smiling again. "To be honest, I did mean to interrupt your thoughts. You appear to be troubled."

I looked at the woman with the brown skin and beautiful clothes. She was the unfamiliar voice I heard in my head. Her smile was dazzling, making me wonder if she were real or just my imagination.

She rose from her table and sat down across from me. "Hi, my people call me Ursula," she held out her big hand.

I blinked. Ursula? My guardian bear in human form? I was unable to think of anything to say. "Claudia." I blurted out my name.

"Hello, Claudia."

I hesitated but asked, "What tribe are you from?"

"Chippewa, in the southeast." She sipped her tea. "Are you a writer?"

"Yeah, something like that." I thought my answer sounded rude, so I added, "I write song lyrics, that's all."

"What a marvelous gift you have. I've never known a songwriter. Do you sing your own songs?"

"No, I write and sell them to music groups and singers."

"Have I heard any of your songs?"

"I don't know. What type of music do you like?"

"I like songs about survival. Gloria Gaynor's *I Will Survive* is one of my favorites."

"Didn't write that one, too bad, I could've made a lot of money." I laughed, but then realized that Ursula had answered my question on how to start telling the truth. "Um, you told me to start with the basics in telling the truth. How did you know what I was questioning?"

"I'm an intuitive, and I can read other people's thoughts."

"Isn't that like trespassing?"

"Yes, yes it could be seen that way," she laughed, "but I don't do it for self-gratification or money. I do it to help people with their issues." Ursula leaned back in her chair while studying my face.

I felt uncomfortable. Reading my thoughts without my permission seemed too much like prying or even spying. "Don't intuitives have a moral code of decency?"

"You're upset with me, and I've offended you. It's because I know you're struggling and I want to help."

"But I don't even know you. You're a stranger who comes into a coffee shop, sits at my table, then tells me how to tell the truth." I glared at Ursula. "Don't you think that that's really weird?"

"From your perspective, yes, from mine, no." Ursula shrugged her slim but muscled shoulders.

I shook my head. "I don't understand how you can help me when you don't even know me."

"I don't need to know your whole background. I only need to know that you're seeking guidance on how to tell the truth without too much detail or being overdramatic, that's all."

"I wish it were that simple."

"It is," Ursula stated. She stood and then asked, "Can I buy you another coffee?"

"Sure, decaf and cream, thank you."

"Right."

◆◆◆◆◆

I sat at the table with Ursula for two hours. As the morning passed, I began to enjoy her perspective on the issues I was facing with my father; and her words of wisdom were extremely comforting. But the fact that her name was Ursula made me feel apprehensive.

Her eyes were like looking beyond the universe and seeing the hope and joy I never felt before, except when I spoke with Ursula, my guardian bear. I smiled to myself thinking of her. As I watched this new Ursula at the counter getting the coffee, it shocked me to think that she was really Ursula in human form. I had to find out. When she returned to the table, I asked, "Do you speak other languages besides English?"

She cocked her head and looked at me before answering. "I speak several languages, English, German, Spanish, Chinese, French, and Cherokee.

I was stunned at her response. Didn't my other Ursula say the same about the languages she spoke in the exact same way? Yes, I remembered; she said these exact same words.

"Okay, enough of the charades. You're really Ursula, my guardian bear, aren't you?"

Ursula stared into my eyes with such intensity that I thought I offended her this time. Then she smiled as warmth flowed through me in waves.

"Yes, in another form."

I nodded and smiled. "How's your shoulder?"

"Healed perfectly," she simply said.

"I didn't think that guardian angels or bears could be hurt."

"Yes, we hurt. We hurt for and with our humans. If you feel pain, we feel that same pain."

"Wow, I've wished so often to see you again after our time at Banning State Park, but I didn't think it was possible."

"Everything is possible, Claudia. You just need to ask."

"I did! I did several times."

"But you need to ask from your heart, not with your head."

I let her comment soak in. Here I was in my local coffee shop talking with my guardian bear who was now my guardian Chippewa Indian. I closed my eyes and opened them quickly to see if this was another one of my extraordinary dreams. Ursula sat at the table as if this were a common occurrence.

"So, shape-shifting is another one of your powers."

"The Divine Spirit agreed to let me visit you again on the condition that I warn you about your father."

"Warn me? He's in jail right now."

"For now, but his lawyer is crafty. They'll make you and your suicide attempt the issue to take away attention from your father's abuse."

"Ohhhh, how can they do that?" I sorely moaned.

"They will, and you need to be ready."

"I have a really good lawyer, Mary Beth Hart. She practices law in domestic cases. She didn't want to take my case at first."

"Why not?"

"She, she, well, she wasn't sure she could represent me." My eyes slid to my hands on my lap.

"Okay, so why not?"

"Mary Beth knew me in college. We dated for a little while." I struggled with the story. "She was uncomfortable with being physical with a woman."

"That's pretty common. Sometimes women don't see other women as partners for a while."

"Well, she doesn't want my father to know about our brief relationship. She's afraid he would make it an issue in the trial."

"Is it an issue with you?"

"No." I shook my head. "I knew I wasn't the person for her.

"How did you know that?"

"Most of my life I've shied away from long-involved relationships because I didn't want people to know the real truth about me." I glanced out the window while my fingers tapped on my coffee cup.

Ursula reached out with her hand and stopped my tapping fingers. She held them for a moment and then let them go. "She knows everything about you now, I'm sure."

I nodded my head. "Yeah, and Mary Beth wants to remove my father away for good."

"So, she agreed to represent you?"

"And Emma," I inserted.

"Good. She probably had a clear sense of what your father did to you and, probably too, witnessed how hurt you were back then."

Again I nodded. "And now…" was all I could blurt out before the sobs began to choke my throat.

Ursula held my hand for a long moment. "Claudia, she cares for you still. Women don't forget their past loves. Men may but not a woman. You need to trust that she'll do the best job for you and Emma."

I continued to nod to her words. I finally managed to say, "I trust Mary Beth."

"I'll be there in court every day."

Surprised, I raised my head and looked into her eyes. "You will?"

"Yes. People have let you down, but I won't, and neither will the Divine Spirit."

"Thank you, Ursula. Your presence will remind me to tell the truth regardless of the pain it causes me."

"I believe in you, Claudia."

♦ ♦ ♦ ♦ ♦

There was that word again, *believe.*

CHAPTER SIXTEEN

By failing to prepare, you are preparing to fail.
—Benjamin Franklin

The courtroom was crowded with people from my father's congregation, his political buddies from the community, and Daniel, my father's perverted friend. Social workers from county welfare agencies were there to see if the famous "fire-and-brimstone preacher" would be convicted of assault and threats to kill. The crimes of child endangerment, including sexual and physical abuse, and adolescent torture and rape, would not be permitted in court because of the statute of limitations.

Further back in the courtroom, Nita sat next to Ursula, my guardian bear, and now my guardian Chippewa Indian. I knew Nita thought the seat next to her was empty. Ursula told me that I was the only one who could see her. Ursula's invisibility made me smile. Nita must have left directly from work because she was in her blue medical scrubs. Ursula was dressed in a bright-colored blouse and skirt and wore native bracelets and rings. She also wore a bright red scarf stylishly wrapped around her long gray hair. It was strange knowing that Nita could not see Ursula like I could, nor could anyone else in the courtroom.

During the first week of the trial, I sat through hours and hours of interviews to select potential jurors. The process was maddening, and my father's slicked-back, greasy thinned-hair lawyer, Clarence Southerly, did not help either. He was dressed in a pin-striped black Mafia-style suit and argued to the judge how my father could not get a fair trial from all the publicity the case had generated. At one point, he brought a motion to move the court case to another jurisdiction. There was so much back and forth in that courtroom that I became lost in the legal proceedings. I finally breathed again when the decision was made to hold the trial right here, and the jury was selected.

◆◆◆◆◆

In the small courtroom, not like the ones on TV, there were a few rows of wooden benches where most of the onlookers sat. The judge's desk was half the size of courtroom desks on TV, and the witness stand was a worn wooden chair behind a railing.

The bailiff called out, "All rise." He waited and then issued, "Department One of the Minnesota court is now in session. Judge Christopher Buckman presiding. Please be seated."

"Good morning, ladies and gentlemen. Calling the case of the People of the State of Minnesota versus Reverend Stanley Thomas. Are both sides ready?" the judge asked.

Mary Beth Hart stood. "Ready for the People, Your Honor."

Clarence Southerly, my father's attorney stood. "Ready for the defense, Your Honor."

Judge Christopher Buckman called to the clerk. "Will the clerk please swear in the jury?"

"Will the jury please stand and raise your right hand? Do each of you swear that you will fairly try the case before this court and that you will return a true verdict according to the evidence and the instructions of the court, so help you, God? Please say "I do." He waited for jurors to say, 'I do.' "You may be seated."

The prosecuting attorney, Mary Beth Hart, a woman who had practiced law for many years and specialized in child and domestic abuse, stood straight in her light blue pants suit. I trusted her with my life.

"Your Honor and ladies and gentlemen of the jury. The defendant has been charged with the crime of assaulting a physical therapist. The evidence will show that the accused broke the nose of Ms. Nita Bernard. The evidence I present will also prove that the defendant has a history of abuse perpetration and is guilty as charged." Mary Beth sat at her table.

Clarence Southerly stood. "Your Honor and ladies and gentlemen of the jury. Under the law, my client is presumed innocent until proven guilty. During this trial, you will hear fraudulent evidence against my client. You will come to know the truth that Reverend Thomas is an outstanding and prominent citizen in this city. Therefore, my client is not guilty." He sat down.

Judge Buckman then declared, "The prosecution may call its first witness."

Mary Beth rose from her chair. "The People would like to call Ms. Nita Bernard to the stand."

Nita stood and walked over to the witness stand where the bailiff asked if she swore to tell the truth and nothing but the truth.

"Yes, I do." Nita sat.

Mary Beth walked over to Nita.

"Hello, would you please state your full name for the record."

"My name is Nita Norwood Bernard."

"Thank you, Ms. Bernard." Mary Beth walked closer to the witness stand. "Where do you work?"

"I'm a certified physical therapist. I work at Hennepin County Medical Center." Nita's answers were short and formal.

"Do you know Reverend Stanley Thomas?"

"No, except when he interrupted a physical therapy appointment I had with his daughter."

"And when was that?"

"On March 24th of this year."

"Is that all he did was interrupt the session?" Mary Beth coaxed.

"No. He made a few comments to Claudia Matthews and me."

"What did he say?"

"He called us black and white lezzies."

"Did he leave after that?"

"No, he started toward Ms. Matthews as if he was going to hit her."

"Did he hit her?"

"No. When I intervened he punched me in my face."

"Did he cause damage?"

"Yes. He broke my nose and gave me two black eyes."

Mary Beth walked over to the evidence table and held up the x-ray. "I'd like to submit this x-ray as Exhibit 1."

The judge nodded.

"Why did Reverend Thomas do that to you?"

"Because I summoned security to make him leave the therapy room. He wouldn't go, so I requested that the two guards escort him from the hospital."

"Was that the last day you saw him?"

"Until today, yes."

"Thank you, Ms. Bernard." As she walked back to her chair, she stated, "I have no further questions for this witness."

Clarence Southerly, my father's attorney stood. "Ms. Bernard are you a lesbian?"

"Objection, your Honor." Mary Beth sprang from her chair.

"Sustained," the judge peered at the attorney over his wire-rim glasses. "Mr. Southerly, please reframe from these sorts of questions. The witness is not on trial."

Stopped in his tracks, Southerly nodded to the judge and returned to his chair. "No further questions."

◆◆◆◆◆

The trial continued after the lunch break.

"Good afternoon, Dr. Lewis, I have a few questions for you." Mary Beth greeted the doctor.

Dr. Lewis nodded.

"Where do you work?"

"Hennepin County Medical Center."

"And what do you do there?"

"I am an orthopedic surgeon. I specialize in the surgical repair of bones, joints, muscles, and tendons in children and young adults."

"You treated Claudia Matthews when she came to the center, didn't you?

"Yes, I did."

"How many broken bones did you find on Ms. Matthews' x-rays when she was admitted?" Mary Beth handed three x-rays to the jury to review.

"Her collarbone was broken probably from the recent fall, but we found ten broken bones where scar tissue had formed around the breaks. Some of these breaks happened more than once and involved Ms. Matthews' hands, feet, legs, and arms."

"Do you know what caused these breaks?"

"These types of broken bones are most likely caused by childhood activities, like falling off a swing or accidentally getting hit by a baseball bat, but when the breaks are repeated—like Ms. Matthews'—this frequently is a sign of physical abuse and trauma to the body."

"Thank you, Dr. Lewis. I have no further questions, your Honor." Mary Beth sat down.

"Mr. Southerly does the defense have any questions for the witness?" the judge asked.

"Yes, your Honor, we do," Southerly sauntered over to the witness stand. "Dr. Lewis, what is your medical degree in?"

"I have a Doctor of Medicine degree."

"And you testified that you are an orthopedic surgeon specializing in the surgical repair in children and young adults."

"Yes."

"Children and young adults, I see. Why were you in consultation on the Claudia Matthews' case since she is an adult?"

"The x-rays of Ms. Matthews were given to me by her attending physician at the hospital when she was brought in the emergency room. I was asked to examine them."

"And why was that?"

"Ms. Matthew's past injuries were alarming."

"In what way?" Southerly leaned into the witness stand.

"These breaks were outside the realm of accidental injuries. We were concerned that Ms. Matthews had been abused as a child and young adult."

"Could you have made a mistake?" Southerly looked directly at Dr. Lewis. "I mean, these injuries are so old, and you said they could be from falling off a swing; perhaps something else could have caused these breaks."

"Not to my knowledge, no." Dr. Lewis glared directly back at Southerly. "These repeated breaks were made on purpose."

"You're sure about this?"

"Yes. I see thousands of x-rays each year, but I have never seen x-rays as devastating as Ms. Matthews."

"I have two hospital reports from emergency visits Ms. Matthews and her mother made to the emergency room at the hospital. Exhibit A and B. Have you seen these, Dr. Lewis?"

"Yes, I have."

"Did you also see where it states in the reports that Ms. Matthews fell while roller skating and hit a parked car with her bike?"

"Yes, I saw these statements." Dr. Lewis shook her head. "Roller skating and bike accidents don't cause these types of breaks."

Southerly frowned at the doctor. "What about other injuries to Ms. Matthews when she was at the state park earlier this year?"

"Ms. Matthews had a gash above her left eyebrow and her collarbone was broken."

"Were Miss Matthews's injuries self-inflicted?"

"Her collarbone injury resulted from a fall off a cliff, or possibly from hitting her head and neck on a stone ledge."

"Why is that, Dr. Lewis?"

"Because Banning State Park is the site of a former stone quarry, these projections can often be found along the Kettle River. There are large stone slabs with very sharp edges. Moss covering these slabs, and in this case snow and ice, can make these extremely dangerous."

"What about the gash on her forehead?"

"The gash was created by what I believe was a bullet." Dr. Lewis' face lacked expression.

Sitting back, I knew that Southerly wanted Dr. Lewis to say that I was crazy, and all the abuse was in my head.

"Where did the bullet come from?" Southerly sneered.

"Most likely from a gun." Laughter rippled through the courtroom. The judge banged his gavel on the desk.

"Dr. Lewis, in your professional opinion, did Ms. Matthews try to kill herself?"

"Objection, your Honor, there is no foundation for this questioning."

"Counsel," the judge turned toward Southerly with one eyebrow raised.

"Your Honor, I'm following up on Dr. Lewis' statement that the injury was caused by a bullet."

Mary Beth said, "Dr. Lewis is an orthopedic surgeon, not a psychiatrist."

"Sustained."

I smiled.

"Thank you, Dr. Lewis. I have no further questions, your Honor." Southerly sat down and whispered in my father's ear. My father lowered his eyes to the floor.

◆◆◆◆◆

"Would you state your name please for the court?" Mary Beth asked my sister.

"I'm Emma Margaret Thomas."

"How are you related to Reverend Thomas?"

"He is my father."

"Are you related to Claudia Matthews?"

"Yes."

"How?"

"She is one of my sisters.

"Thank you. Emma. How would you describe your childhood?" Mary Beth tried to reduce my little sister's anxiousness.

"It was chaotic at best," she said simply.

"Can you be more specific for us?

"My parents fought all the time, so my brothers and sisters tried to spend as little time at home."

"What did your parents fight about?"

"My father spent a lot of time at the church or visiting people in the congregation. My mother was at home, cooking, cleaning, doing laundry, and trying to keep five children in line. She was always exhausted."

"Did you ever see your father physically harm your mother?"

"No, only the bruising and lost teeth afterward."

"Objection, your Honor." Southerly pounded the table. "This is purely speculation."

"Your Honor, this witness' answers validate that physical harm was common in the family."

"Overruled."

"Go on, Emma," Mary Beth consoled her as she walked over to the jury.

"I overheard my mom and dad fighting right before her teeth got knocked out."

"You heard your father and mother arguing?"

"Yes."

"Did you ever see injuries on Claudia?"

Emma looked across the room at me in apology. She lowered her eyes. "Yes."

"Do you know how Claudia got hurt?"

"No, Claudia never talked about how she got hurt." Em peered down at her hands.

"Did that strike you as odd?"

"No."

"Why not?"

"Claudia protected us. She always stepped in between our father and us. If he raised his hand to any of us, Claudia would take the hit."

"But I thought you said you never saw your father hit Claudia, and now you say he did. Will you clear up this confusion for the jury, Emma?"

"Father never hit Claudia in front of us. He would take her down to the basement and hit her. Claudia would come back upstairs with a cut on her lip or her nose would be bleeding."

"How often did this occur where your father would take Claudia down to the basement?"

"I'd estimate every other week."

"That's a lot of time, wouldn't you say, Emma?"

"Yes, an eternity," she mumbled, trying to hold back her tears.

The courtroom was silent and filled with tension. People looked at one another with shock on their faces.

"Emma," Mary Beth continued after this painfilled pause. "The day before your mother died, she gave you a box, isn't that correct?"

"Yes, she did," Emma glanced at me and added, "five months ago."

Mary Beth quickly moved to a table and lifted a box wrapped in brown paper. One side of it was open.

"I'm showing you what has been marked as Exhibit C. Do you recognize this, Emma?"

"Yes."

"How do you recognize it?"

"It's the box my mother gave me which I gave to you prior to this trial.

"What is it?"

"I don't know. My mother told me not to open it. It was Claudia's."

"Is this box in substantially the same condition as when you gave it to me?"

"Yes."

"Your Honor, I offer Exhibit C into evidence."

"Counsel?" asked the judge.

"No objection, your Honor," said my father's lawyer.

"The Exhibit is received." The judge returned to his notes.

Mary Beth raised the box in front of Em. "So, this is the box she gave you?"

"Yes," Emma slowly nodded.

"When your mother gave you this box, did she know she was dying?"

"Objection, your Honor. This information is not relevant to this case."

"Sustained," the judge replied.

"It was the day before she died. Mom told me not to open it, but to give it to Claudia if she was ever in trouble."

"What kind of trouble?"

"Mom never said." Emma looked directly at me. "I knew the box contained evidence of Claudia's abuse, but I never looked inside."

"You never gave this box to Claudia. Why is that?"

"I knew it would cause Claudia to remember what Father did to her. I didn't want her to remember being hurt."

"Thank you, Emma.

Southerly rose and buttoned his suit coat. He coughed. "May I call you Emma?"

Emma nodded.

"So you said you never saw your father hit Claudia, is that correct, Emma?"

"Yes."

"Did you see Claudia's injuries?"

"Yes. Her left arm was broken twice. Her right leg was also broken. Claudia had several black eyes and bruises on her face and neck. She often had severe cramping in her stomach."

"Was this due to menstruation?"

"Sometimes, but not always."

"What do you mean by sometimes?" Southerly stood directly in front of Emma.

"Claudia and I often had our periods at the same time. But her cramping came from blows to her stomach."

"How do you know this?"

"Claudia was often bent over her stomach even when she didn't have her period."

"Did she say she was ever punched in the stomach?"

"Not to me." Emma looked at me. "She may have told a friend. Claudia didn't like to frighten me."

"No more question for this witness," Southerly said as he sat down.

Emma rose and walked to where I was sitting behind the prosecutor's table. She gave me a hug and whispered, "I'm so sorry, Claudia."

◆◆◆◆◆

"Please state your name for the court," Mary Beth strolled toward the stand where a middle-aged man sat sporting a wide and thick Chevron mustache. He wore it long to cover the top of his upper lip.

"Frank Messinger."

"What do you do, Mr. Messinger?"

"I'm a forensic science technician at the Hennepin County Crime lab."

"What is your job?"

"Forensic science technicians play an important role in a laboratory, as we ensure that evidence is not compromised and that the rules and regulations within the lab are followed at all times. Our duties help forensic scientists conduct crime tests and analyses in a timely fashion."

Mary Beth stood in front of the technician and lifted a clear plastic bag out of the box. She raised the bag to eye level. "Did you assist in the analysis of this pair of a teenager's underwear?"

"Yes."

"Ladies and gentlemen of the jury, I'd like to present Exhibit C. This pair of underwear belonged to the former Claudia Thomas and current Claudia Matthews. Mr. Messinger you analyzed this pair of underwear, didn't you?"

"Yes I did. I tested and results reveal Claudia's blood and Reverend Thomas' semen."

Mary Beth returned the underwear to the box and laid it on the evidence table, then she turned to the judge. "Those are all my questions for this witness, your Honor." She took a step and stopped looking at the judge. "With this DNA exhibit, the people now ask that this trial include the offense of numerous episodes of child abuse along with the other mentioned crimes."

"I hereby add child abuse to the list of crimes." The judge asked. "Does the defense have any questions for this witness?"

Red-faced, Southerly mustered to say, "No."

Within seconds, the courtroom suddenly became hot and stuffy and I felt dizzy and unable to move in my chair. I stared at the plastic bag and box on the evidence table. I suddenly remembered the huge tantrum I threw at the age of nine or ten when I could not find my favorite pair of underwear. When I asked my mother if she knew where my underwear was, she told me that they had a rip in them and had to be thrown away. I continued with my incensed tantrum until my father grabbed me by my arm and dragged me to the basement. The punishment was savage.

The truth slapped me in the face.

My mother knew about the abuse long before she told me. I could feel the heat of anger burn my stomach and throat. I peered at my clenched fists trying to hide the betrayal and resentment I felt for my mother at this moment. The emotional pain seared through my body, mind, and spirit like radioactive rays, while my head buzzed with a growing migraine. I closed my eyes to shut out the memories of my mother, but I could not shut off the anger. I felt myself collapse where I was sitting and heard a loud bang when my head hit the chair in front of me.

◆ ◆ ◆ ◆ ◆

A day later, I was sitting in the witness stand with a medium-sized black bruise on my forehead. I pledged to tell the whole truth and nothing but the whole damned truth, so help me Father. My hands trembled, although I did not feel nervous, but the ache in my head had the potential of becoming a migraine. Luckily for me, courtrooms were known for their gloomy ambiance and low lighting. The chair I was perched on was hard on my butt. Therefore, I could not find a comfortable position.

The prosecuting attorney, Mary Beth Hart, began her questioning with some simple answers I could provide.

"Claudia, how are you today?"

"I'm okay, maybe a bit anxious."

"That's to be expected. I'd like to start out with a few quick questions for you."

I nodded.

"You are the third child of Stanley and Rachel Thomas, correct?"

"Yes."

"Why is your last name different than your father's?"

"I changed my name five years ago to Matthews, my mother's maiden name."

"Your mother is deceased?"

"Yes, she died last November."

"Do you know how she died?"

"She fell down the basement stairs and hit her head on the concrete floor."

"Where you there?"

"No, I was not."

"Who told you about her fall?"

"My sister, Emma," and then I added, "she called me that day."

"Do you know if your father abused your mother?"

"Objection, your Honor," Clarence Southerly stood up immediately. "There's been no foundation for this."

"Your Honor," Mary Beth shouted, "I'm trying to establish a pattern of abuse in the family."

"Go on," the judge said. Southerly sat down shaking his head and grumbling.

"Claudia, I'll repeat my question, did your father abuse your mother?"

"Yes."

The people in the courtroom began to talk, raising the sound level in the room.

"Order in the court," the judge demanded as he hit the gavel on his desk.

"Yes?" Mary Beth asked me.

"Yes, absolutely," I replied.

"And how do you know this?"

"I saw her bruises and cuts."

"Did he hurt anyone else in the family?"

"Yes," I tried to calm my nerves.

"Who?"

"Me." I slowly inhaled a breath of stuffy air. "I was a child. I remembered being spanked by him."

"How old were you when this spanking started?"

"Around the age of five."

"Did this happen frequently when you were a child?"

"Yes."

"Did your father spank your brothers and sisters, too?"

"No, if they did something wrong, he would spank me."

"He spanked you instead of your siblings? Do you know why he did this to you?"

"No."

"Did the spankings stop?"

"No, not until I was around the age of nine or ten."

Mary Beth looked at me with sadness in her eyes. "What happened when the spankings stopped?"

"My father started to hit and kick me." I could feel the tears stinging my eyes. It was so emotionally draining for me to review the past. I wiped away the tears. "When I was young, he'd hit and slap me on my body and head. He'd yell at me and call me names like stupid and ugly." I paused, trying to stop myself from shaking, but it was impossible. I continued, "As I grew older the hits and slaps turned into punches and leg kicks." I coughed and cleared my throat. "When I was ten, he started to make me touch his genitals. Then he would touch mine. Then he would put his fingers in me," I gasped. I heard a collective groan in the courtroom. "Then he would shove his penis into me. It hurt so bad, but when I screamed, he simply pushed harder. I was only thirteen by this time, but despite my pleas for him to stop, he wouldn't."

"Your father wouldn't stop. Then what did he do?" Mary Beth asked.

"He began to use his belt." I could feel the growing tension in my brothers and sisters sitting behind me. They were all present except for Judith who was still in the psych ward at the hospital. "He also would burn me with his cigars."

"His cigars? You mean he burned your skin with his cigars?"

"Yes." I stopped. The sudden smell of burning flesh caused the bile in my throat to move into my mouth. I lowered my head. The painful memory was unbearable.

"Claudia, do you need a break?" The tone of Mary Beth's question was so kind.

I shook my head. "The burns were extremely painful."

"Claudia will you please stand and show the jury both of your arms?"

I did as Mary Beth asked.

When I rolled up my sleeves for the jury to see the scars, several people on the jury gasped. The scars were deep, round, and pink. Numerous scars appeared on the inside of both of my arms.

"Thank you, Claudia, you can pull your sleeves down." Mary Beth pointed to the screen behind me. "Claudia, directing your attention to the picture on the screen, do you recognize this picture?"

"Yes."

"Tell the jury what this photo depicts."

"This is a photo of my stomach."

"How do you recognize this as a picture of your stomach?"

"As you can see, there are cigar burns on the left and right sides of my belly button, as well as right below my left ribs. I recognize this pattern as the scarring on my stomach."

"Does this photo accurately depict the scars on your abdomen?"

"Yes."

"Your Honor, I'm offering this photo as Exhibit D."

"Any objection?" the judge asked the defense.

"No, your Honor," Southerly said.

"Exhibit D is received," stated the judge.

A woman stood up in the audience and fainted, falling to the floor. Several other people helped the unconscious woman out of the room.

"I have no further questions for Claudia, your Honor."

"Defense, are you ready to question the witness?"

"Yes, we are your Honor." Southerly stood up from his chair at the defense table and raised his notebook. He looked at his notes and stood directly in front of me. "You stated in the papers filed with the court that your father, Reverend Stanley Thomas, traumatized you several times. What are the exact dates?"

I blinked. It never occurred to me that I would be asked about specific dates. I wanted to cry. "I can't remember all the dates."

"You have accused your father of doing horrendous things to you, but you can't remember the dates?"

"There were so many times he hurt me, and he started when I was very young."

"Objection, your Honor," Mary Beth cut in. "The defense is badgering the witness."

"Sustained. Mr. Southerly, move along." Judge Buckman looked at me.

"Yes, your Honor." Southerly moved over to the table and conferred with his assistant. "Miss Matthews, I have a few more questions for you."

I took a deep breath in and exhaled slowly. "Is this really happening?" I asked myself. I still could not believe that my father had done these cruel things, yet he had been arrested only for assaulting Nita. But with the evidence of my dirtied underwear, the case had become more grueling.

As hard as it was to believe, and now admit, the man who had abused me was not a stranger, not a boyfriend nor a husband—it was my father, one man above all men who should have unconditionally loved and protected me. Again those two words: Why me?

My father was dressed in an orange jumpsuit, and his hair was closely shaved. He was also very thin. I had noticed this the day before when the trial began but did not see him since he broke into my house and threatened to kill Emma and me.

"When was the last time you saw your father?" Southerly asked.

"A month ago when he broke into my house and tried to stab my sister and me."

"Did he actually say he was going to kill you?"

"Yes, and he told me to save my sister, Emma."

"Do you know if your father had been drinking?"

"Yes, his breath wreaked of beer and cigar smoke." I closed my eyes trying to forget the scene. I could feel my heart bleeding.

"Do you have any reason your father supposedly attacked you that day? Did you do something? Had you argued with your father? Did you make him angry?"

"Objection, your Honor, the defense is badgering the witness again. The witness is not on trial here."

"Sustained," the judge barked.

"I will again ask my first question. Do you have any reason your father supposedly attacked you that day?

I shook my head, no. "I have never done anything to Stanley to make him hurt me so much and so often."

"You refer to your father as Stanley, his proper name. You don't call him father or dad?"

"No, he's not my father."

"But your birth certificate states that he is your biological father, yes?"

"Biological for his sperm, but little else."

"Claudia, children test their parents. Are you saying that you never tested your parents or made them angry with you?"

"What my father did to me isn't a question of anger; it's a question of rage and madness."

Clarence Southerly raised his bushy eyebrows at my comment. "Rage and madness? Oh, Miss Matthews, your father is a man of God sworn to protect and give comfort to his flock."

"Objection, your Honor, Mr. Southerly is trying to intimidate the witness."

I could still taste the sour bile in my throat. I wanted to scream.

"Sustained. Mr. Southerly, would you reframe your question for the witness?"

"Miss Matthews, is there any chance you created some of this drama to get attention?" Southerly looked at me. "None of your brothers or sisters were hurt. Why did he single you out?"

"They all know what Stanley did to me and were afraid that if they said anything, he would turn on them." I looked out at the people in the courtroom. "My sister Emma has already testified to this fact."

"But how would we know if you and your sister Emma acted together and planned 'this little drama'?"

"Objection, your Honor," Mary Beth yelled, "The defense is asking the witness argumentative questions."

Southerly looked at the judge and smiled.

"Sustained."

I was simmering in my own rage. How could Southerly really think Emma and I dreamed this up. When my fingers curled in, the urge to strike him was enormous. But, no, that would be what my father would do. I stole a minute to calm myself, reminding me *that I am not my father.* I sat back in my chair and inhaled several deep breaths.

"Miss Matthews, as I understand your testimony, you have no dates of abuse, no witnesses to your supposed abuse, and no support in the form of any of your brothers or sisters being abused, is that about right?"

"Mr. Southerly, I have never made up any of Stanley's abuse. He is responsible, he is totally responsible for breaking my bones, torturing, and raping me, burning me with his cigars, and robbing me of my childhood. I am not to blame for his evil ways. He is and always will be responsible for what he did to me."

My words hung in the silence of the courtroom. No one moved or talked. I grabbed on to the wooden rail in front of me, lowered my head, and began to sob.

I heard the judge bang his gavel on the desk. "This court is adjourned and will resume tomorrow sharply at 9 a.m."

CHAPTER SEVENTEEN

*Choosing to generate and flow unconditional love is
the only permanent way to end suffering.*
—Dan Brulé

When I heard the doorbell ring, I walked to the door and looked through the peephole. Nita stood on my porch with a beautiful smile on her face. I opened the door.

"Hi," I smirked. "I don't remember ordering pizza."

"Special delivery for the brave."

I stood aside as Nita walked into my apartment and set the pizza box on the dining room table.

"The brave?"

"Yes, the brave." Nita opened the box. The savory smell of cheese and sausage wafted through the room. A bottle of wine appeared from under her arm. "Glasses?"

"I'm on it," I closed the door and entered the kitchen to retrieve two wine glasses. Returning to the dining room, I looked directly into Nita's eyes. They were so dark brown they reminded me of Ursula's. "Is this for my dramatic scene today in court?"

Nita wrapped her arms around me. The scent of her hair smelled so fresh, and I felt myself falling deeper into her strong arms.

"Claudia, I'm so sorry for all the pain and suffering you've been through because of your father. I could hardly breath today when I saw you crying on the witness stand."

"Dramatic, huh?"

"Ultimately, traumatic is more like it." Nita ushered me into a chair and placed a piece of pizza on my plate. She then retrieved a bottle opener out of her pocket and popped the cork. Nita poured two classes of the Mateus Portuguese Rosé, my all-time favorite. She handed me a glass. "If had known what your father was doing to you, I would've cut off his penis."

Wine spurted out through my nose and mouth. "You what?"

"Indeed, I would've dumped that bastard into a steel barrel, put the lid on tight, and drummed him to death."

"That's stickin' it to him, Nita."

"Cute, but not the issue." Nita bit into her pizza. Some pizza sauce appeared on her upper lip. I wiped it off with my finger. "Thanks."

"I can only imagine how many people in that courtroom were thinking about similar scenarios." The wine wound down my throat, feathering warmth and floral scents into my stomach.

"Claudia, how were you able to endure all of his torture for so long? Didn't you want to kill him?" Nita's eyes were wide.

I smiled. "Yes, but then I would've been just like him. Every action he took, I did the opposite. I didn't want to be like him."

"After these last few days in court, I can totally understand this." Nita paused. "Your wounds and scars are so—"

"Ugly!" I interjected.

"No, Claudia, no. Your wounds and scars tell a story of what happens when you had to fight evil. They are badges of courage and resilience."

"Hmmm, I think I like your description better than my own." I bit into my pizza and then took a sip of wine. "OMG! This pizza and wine are so amazingly yummy. Thanks for bringing it over. I'm so glad you're here."

This time, Nita wiped some sauce off my face with her finger and then eased it into her mouth. "Now it's even better." She winked at me.

I smiled again. "I will never be able to thank you enough for being in court these past few days. I'm sure I'd have reacted differently if you hadn't been present."

"Different, how so?"

I shrugged, saying, "I'm not sure, but I'm grateful you are here for me."

Nita grasped my hand and squeezed it. "I wouldn't be anywhere else."

I picked up my wine glass and walked over to the couch and sat down. I patted the seat next to me. Nita rose from her chair and closed the box of pizza. She brought the bottle of wine with her to the couch and refilled my glass.

"Are you trying to get me drunk?"

Nita shook her head. "No, but I wanted to give you a chance to relax and be in the moment. Your mind and body have been stretched beyond limit, and I want you to be here with me and enjoy this time."

When I examined my hands holding the wine glass, I could feel tears beginning to surface. I did not want to cry in front of Nita, but when I glanced up at her there were tears in her eyes. The dam broke, and my heart flooded with an unknown feeling.

"Is this love?" I silently questioned.

Nita grasped my glass and placed it on the coffee table. Then she brought her arms around me and caught me in a bear hug. "Claudia, I knew there was something special about you. In high school, I used to watch you caring for other students. You sat in the cafeteria with students who were sitting by themselves. You friended everyone, including me."

"But you were so popular. You always had a group of people around you."

"You can be alone in a crowd, you know that Claudia."

"You mean you were as lonely as me?"

Nita nodded. "I knew I was a lesbian, but I was so afraid my family and friends would learn the truth. Being black and a lesbian isn't exactly a winning combination." She released her hold on me, reached over my body, and took a sip of her wine. "I was the only black person in our school until Melvin came. But he was a basketball wonder, and students loved him. I was but another girl in the band."

"Okay, I have a confession. I watched you, too."

"You did? I never noticed." Nita breathed. "Why?"

"I think in some ways I knew you and I had a lot in common. It was a feeling I had. I loved my mother and siblings, but I never knew what feeling love was like for a person outside of my family. I was so unaccustomed to this new feeling."

"Me too."

"So, when I realized I had fallen in love with you, I ran away from that feeling."

"Had?" Nita smirked.

"Okay, have. Is that better?"

Nita kissed the top of my head. "You don't ever need to run away again." She shifted her body and faced me. "If I had my bongo drums, I could beat what my heart feels, but expressing them in words is difficult for me. I had to learn."

"Your sense of rhythm is beyond beautiful." I coughed. "And so is your sense of style and speech." I was becoming uncomfortable.

"Thank you. Hey, are you embarrassed?"

"Yeah, I feel like I could open my whole life to you, but the fear of you thinking of me as a bad person would crush me."

"Not to worry," Nita smiled. "And I'm fearful you won't like me when I tell you my story."

"Okay, so we're even. You mentioned before that you had to learn how to express your feelings without the bongos. How?"

"I met a woman in college who made me feel like a million bucks. Unfortunately, she was such a fake. And then she robbed me of a million bucks."

"Really! A million dollars?"

"Well, it wasn't a million, but it felt like it after she used me to feed her spending addiction."

"Oh, Nita, I'm so sorry."

"I gave her my heart and soul, and then she abandoned me after I had to file bankruptcy. God, I was so angry. I promised myself that I would never ever fall in love again. But I did. This time the feelings were mutual, but then Haley died from cancer."

"Oh no. I'm so sorry." I felt so stunned that I could not think of comforting words to say."

"We had six years of bliss. Haley taught me how to express my feelings in a verbal way. She was such a great communicator. My heart and soul learned to love unconditionally. And when she became sick, I didn't think I could survive without her."

"But you did. How long ago did she die?"

"Four years ago." Nita took another sip of wine. "I returned to school and finished a degree in physical therapy. I need to help others find the strength they possess to walk again."

"Like me?"

"Yes, like you." Nita closed her eyes. "I remember your first day of therapy. You looked so uncomfortable with that halo brace on."

"I was. That thing hurt."

"You'd never know you had a brace looking at you now."

"Good thing. Did you know that my father arrived at the hospital and tried to twist the brace?"

"Shit, yeah! I was so angry that I wanted to cut off his penis with a dull knife."

I laughed. "You sure have an obsession for cutting off penises."

"Did you know that black women suffer from incest nearly two times more than white women?"

"Seriously? I didn't know that." I thought for a moment. "Yikes, you weren't abused as a child, were you?"

Nita shook her head. "I had friends who were." She shivered and added, "I wanted to help these girls out so much, but I didn't know how. And now hearing your story, I realize that women of all colors are abused. Makes me livid."

"Me too." The two of us grew silent.

"Listen, Claudia, I should get going. It's getting late, and you have another day in court."

I panicked as Nita rose from the couch. "No, wait!" Tears began to roll down my cheeks.

"What's wrong, Claudia?" Nita wrapped me in her arms again.

"Please stay with me tonight?" I hesitated. "I want to fall asleep in your arms."

Nita held my head in her hands and lifted my face. "Are you scared?"

"Yeah, like hell." I whimpered.

"Well, it so happens that I'm free tonight and would love to protect you." Nita kissed me on my forehead.

"No sex," I mumbled, feeling my cheeks redden.

"No sex. It would be my honor to hold you close for a few hours."

"Thank you."

CHAPTER EIGHTEEN

The truth will set you free, but
first it will make you miserable.
—James A. Garfield

That night I lay in bed with Nita reviewing my testimony. There
were so many incidents that I could have stated but did not. I
chastised myself for not remembering specific details. How could
I have forgotten that my father would tie me down to the old
mattress in the basement? How could I forget how much anger
there was in his eyes? How could I forget that he would threaten
me by telling me that he would kill my mother if I ever said a word
to anyone? My thoughts raced.

Deciding it was futile to try to sleep, I slowly got out of bed,
set off for the kitchen, and brewed myself some herbal tea. The
chamomile filled my nose with a soothing smell as I steadily drank
the hot liquid.

"Claudia, you're now at a point where, if you truly want to live, you have
to be who you are," Dr. Sloan had said this to me at my last therapy
session.

"She's right," I said to myself.

There was no time for denial. Father was arrested, and his trial
was about over. People from his congregation claimed he was a
good man, a man of faith. Not only did he help them in their hour
of need, but he also helped deepen their faith in God. His church
fed the starving, and he had mattresses in the church's basement
for the homeless. He did do good work for his church, but not for
this child…

I knew I would never understand my father or why he did what he did, but I figured he would be sentenced to three years in prison, he would have to register as a sex offender, he would lose all parental rights, and his reputation would be ruined. But was this enough to punish him for his actions?

"Enough?" I laughed at myself, not wanting to wake Nita. Was there a sentence that would fit the crimes he committed? I shook my head. No, my father was going to go on living, but he would lose his freedom. F-r-e-e-d-o-m. I focused on the word. "Freedom, he will lose his freedom." I wrote the word on a napkin.

Next to freedom, I wrote the word punishment. I blinked at the word at first, but then held my gaze on it. While I was thinking about what my father's sentence would entail, I subconsciously thought of the word 'punishment.' Next came the word 'Compassion.'

Freedom. Punishment. Compassion. I rolled my head from side to side. What were these words saying? Did they relate to one another? Did they have a purpose? Did they have a meaning?

The words blended and separated, swirled, dived, and exploded. My mind whirled around, searching for a meaning. "What do I know about each of these words?" I wondered.

Freedom. My own freedom growing up had been taken away from me. I could not do any activities or go places without letting my parents know what I was undertaking. My wings were clipped so I could not fly. Every evening at the dinner table, father asked each of us who we had talked to that day and what was said. He wanted to know everything that we did each hour of the day. Now looking back, I realized that he was keeping tabs on each of us. He wanted to know if we spoke about him to our friends or teachers. He wanted to know if we cursed him or were angry with him. He wanted, more than life, to cut us off from the people we might turn to for help. At many dinners, my mother would try to intervene with his questions, but father would turn to her and glare. The look in his eyes was frightening, and I know we all felt scared. In response, we told him all about our studies and our friends. He visibly handcuffed us to our chairs, and he would not release us until he was satisfied with our answers. On days I refused to answer his questions, he brought me down into the basement and punished me.

Punishment. I was always being punished for actions I did or did not do. The methods were different, each punishment was worse than the one before. As I described in court, punishment went from spankings to kicking to sexual abuse. My father knew that punishment, or the threat of punishment, was a way to control the behaviors of his wife and children. I paused for a moment.

"Isn't punishment the foundation of our criminal justice system?" I nodded to the quiet room.

Never fearing that he would be punished for his treatment of my mother or me, he continually experimented with how much pain mom or I could bear. His belief that he would never get caught made him bold. He was not afraid of his children or wife, and he had no fear of monsters because he was one. I know he never considered himself a monster.

"Was he physically and sexually abused when he was a child?" The room was perfectly quiet. I shuddered. A chill went down my spine as I remembered Emma's words.

"Yes, he was abused as a young man," my sister Emma had stated a long time ago. "Child abuse is intergenerational, occurring every generation after generation. Abuse is a horrible cycle that needs professional help to stop, and we need the entire U.S. legal system to eliminate child abuse."

I remembered how I thought Emma had become a good and enlightened psychologist. I never asked her how she knew about father's abuse. She said he had all the classic behaviors and symptoms. I had forgotten Emma's words until now.

I dropped my head into my hands as the tears trickled down my cheeks.

My father had been physically and sexually abused, too. The thought made me shiver. I would have thought that this fact would make me less angry, but it did not. I could feel my cheeks grow hot as I threw the pen across the room and crumpled the napkin with the three words on it.

"How can I feel sorry for him?" I suddenly remembered the words Ursula said to me while we were sitting around the campfire.

"You didn't ask to be abused, Claudia. You did nothing to cause the abuse."

"And neither did my father." I sat back in my chair. I pictured my father as a young man, handsome and charming. At least that was what Mom had said. But another man took that charm away, and a monster was born.

"Am I a monster?" I silently observed. "No, no way! I don't hurt other people or animals. I could never—"

I closed my tired eyes against the pain.

"It comes down to choices," Dr. Sloan had stated when I saw her for therapy while in the hospital. *"When children are abused, they have the choice to do the same to their future children or not. Claudia, your father perpetuated this evil cycle by abusing you and your mom."*

I remember feeling so frightened when Dr. Sloan made this statement.

"You mean, I could choose to abuse my children if I had them?" I shamefully questioned Dr. Sloan.

"Yes, if that's what you had chosen. But Claudia, you didn't choose that behavior."

"Why didn't I?"

"Because you have compassion for yourself and others." Her words were etched into my soul.

Compassion.

Out of the darkness, it appeared, the last word on the list I made tonight.

So now I knew I needed to show compassion to myself before I could show compassion to others, including my father. Ewwww, this was going to be hard. Yet, I also knew that giving compassion to myself was where I could start healing. And maybe, someday, I would have compassion for my father. Was this even possible?

"Can I offer compassion to that abused young man without forgiving him?" My head began to spin. I could not believe the next words out of my mouth, "I'm sorry, Father, that you were abused. You didn't deserve it, and you're not to blame."

I left the dining room, got back in bed, and snuggled up to Nita who was peacefully sleeping.

"Yes, I am truly sorry for you, Stanley, but I can't forgive you for choosing to perpetuate this sinful cycle. The abuse stops with me, but it hasn't for you. You had a choice, and you blew it. And for what? What did you gain? You didn't gain anything, and now you've lost your freedom."

The phrase, *"I'm sorry, Stanley,"* kept repeating in my mind.

As I closed my eyes, I finally realized the truth. My life had been miserable to this point, but though I had been unfairly and horribly abused, *I was now consciously choosing freedom and compassion.*

◆◆◆◆◆

The next day, Mary Beth Hart made her closing statements.

"I want to remind the jury that Reverend Thomas assaulted a physical therapist at the hospital, who oversaw Claudia Matthews's recovery. He also is charged with breaking and entering Claudia's apartment. And, as we've seen and heard, his punishment of Claudia falls under 'cruel and unusual punishment.' These are ALL criminal offenses."

"Ladies and gentlemen of the jury, this story of abuse and child endangerment is beyond comprehension. How can a father, a revered evangelical minister, inflict hideous corporal punishment on one of his children over decades, and expect to return to his duties of his church? Thirty-one nations fully ban corporal punishment in homes, schools, and churches. One serious exception is the United States."

She paused to let her words sink in.

"Countless studies prove that there is a common denominator among those who abuse children. They seek out situations where they have easy access and cover. The church is, therefore, the perfect community to attract people with a strong sexual interest in children. It should surprise no human being that an abuser is a minister, priest, or rabbi."

Mary Beth held up three x-rays to the jury.

"I use the word hideous to describe Claudia's punishment, and you'll recall seeing the x-rays ordered by Dr. Lewis to determine the extent of damage done to Claudia's neck when she fell. As we heard, Dr. Lewis was shocked to find that there was evidence that Claudia had ten broken bones, some of which were broken repeatedly. The jury will remember that the x-rays showed hard calluses, hard bumps that formed around a fracture when a bone is broken and healing. These injuries were not due to her fall several months ago. They were broken year after year beginning at the age of five.

"Again, the jury will remember that Claudia displayed to us more than fifteen scars on her skin, scars made by cigar burns. The defense will tell you that Reverend Thomas chose to discipline in these hideous ways and will continue to argue because he believes Claudia is 'supposedly' mentally ill because she is a lesbian. Ladies and gentlemen, Claudia is a self-identified lesbian. Before 1973, homosexuality was actually considered a 'mental illness,' at least by the psychiatrists that authored the second edition of the Diagnostic and Statistical Manual of Mental Disorders (DSM-II). In the third edition, homosexuality was reclassified as a normal state of being. More recently, in 2013, the Supreme Court made marriage between two people of the same sex legal. Being a lesbian is neither a crime in the United States, nor is it a sign of mental illness.

"With all the corporal punishment Claudia Matthews has received at the hands of Reverend Thomas, we would think that she would be mentally ill, but she is not. Claudia is intelligent and well educated. She has emotionally coped with such brutality over the years without showing any signs of retribution. She has never once physically hurt her father. He has no broken bones or scars on his flesh. It amazes me that Claudia is so sane.

"Can we allow this supposed man of God to torture and beat his child without reprimand?"

She picked up an official-looking binder and read the contents and quoted,

> The following statistics come from the American Society for the Positive Care of Children. American children are suffering from a hidden epidemic of child abuse and

neglect. National child abuse estimates are well known for being under-reported. This is a report from *The Children's Bureau* and published in January 2017. The report shows an increase in child abuse referrals from 3.6 million to 4 million. The report also indicates an increase in child deaths from abuse and neglect to 1,670 in 2015, up from 1,580 in 2014. Some reports estimate child abuse fatalities at 1,740 or even higher today.

The United States has one of the worst records among industrialized nations, losing on average almost five children every day to child abuse and neglect.

She placed the binder on the table and stepped over to the jury.

"Ladies and gentlemen, can we let men like Reverend Thomas freely abuse and neglect our children? Absolutely not. Our children are our future. If this atrocious, appalling, cruel, and unusual treatment continues without punishment, we have no future."

Mary Beth hung her head, paused, and slowly looked up at the jury.

"However you decide to punish Reverent Stanley Thomas, that punishment will never equal the immoral and perpetual punishment and torture he brought to his wife, Rachel, and his child, Claudia Matthews.

◆◆◆◆◆

The next day, Clarence Southerly made his closing statements.

"Ladies and gentlemen of the jury, we've had the opportunity to explore the relationship between Reverend Stanley Thomas and his daughter, Claudia. By no means is this relationship ideal. Reverend Thomas has been a minister for more than four decades. His devotion to God and his church community has been exemplar. He continues to help the homeless and the poor in our city. How can a man with such kindness be the vicious monster that Claudia Matthews portrays him?"

I saw Mary Beth stand up to object, but then slowly sat down. I could not believe what I was hearing.

"Reverend Thomas' job as a minister has a lot of stress with long hours, depressed and dying congregation members, births and weddings, a family of five children, and a sick and now deceased wife. Does he get upset at times? Yes! Does he lose his cool at times? Yes. Is he exhausted? Yes. Does he make mistakes? Yes. Is he human like you and me? Yes. Does this make him a criminal? No."

Southerly turned and looked from the judge to the jury.

"Members of the jury, is life perfect? No, it's not. Life is filled with unintentional moments that we regret and wish we could take back. Reverend Thomas feels this way. He never meant to hurt Claudia, but because she is mentally ill, it is difficult to love her. But Reverend Thomas did and tried his best to deal with her lesbianism. It was her mental illness that fabricated the lies and stories you heard in this courtroom. And, it was her mental illness that led her to try and take her own life."

"Objection, your Honor," Mary Beth stood up. "Counsel is misstating the evidence."

"Overruled," said the judge, "I urge both attorneys not to object during closing statements."

Southerly paused, shook his head from side to side.

"Let the jury be advised that the United States has no laws prohibiting corporal punishment in the home. Under the law, Reverend Thomas did not commit a crime in disciplining his daughter. Particularly in this case, disciplining Claudia for her mental illness, without a doubt, was difficult for Reverend Thomas to do."

Mary Beth stood up but stopped herself from objecting. She had to let Southerly's statement be. She sat down without a word.

Southerly approached the jury.

"I can only imagine the sadness Reverend Thomas felt when he heard his own daughter tried to end her life. Did he respond appropriately upon hearing the news? No. He is her father. He traveled to a bar and tried to forget how difficult a child Claudia has been all her life. He tried to use alcohol to ease the burden of failing his wife and his children. He tried for years to be a good father. He tried for years to give his family a solid home, good food, and nice clothing while he perpetually bore the needs of one of the largest churches in the country. We all know that Reverend Thomas has a demanding boss. God expects his ministers of faith to be pillars of strength, to work more than average men, to lay his life down if called to do so. Yet, here is Claudia, Reverend Thomas' selfish child, accusing him of treating her unfairly. A child who expected and demanded the best. When she didn't get the attention she craved, she drove to Banning State Park to kill herself. Did she fail? Yes, she failed."

I closed my eyes and clenched my fists. I felt Ursula wrap her arms around my shoulders and whisper, "Hold on."

"So, your Honor and members of the jury, should Reverend Thomas be blamed for Claudia's inappropriate actions to harm herself? No. Should he be held responsible for her mental illness? No, I repeat, no!"

He walked in front of the jury with his arms spread.

"Did Reverend Thomas assault the physical therapist in the hospital and threaten his children? Yes, he did and he is willing to be punished. But, I ask the jury to remember that Reverend Thomas is not on trial for child and domestic abuse."

"Yes, he is," Mary Beth yelled.

Southerly smirked and sat down next to my father.

◆◆◆◆◆

I dashed to the women's restroom, where I vomited into the toilet while Nita and Emma tried to talk to me in soothing tones. The staggering number of broken bones and exhibits of torture reported by Dr. Lewis was the truth, and no matter how Clarence Southerly tried to build up his client, the fact remained that Stanley Thomas tortured and abused me throughout my life, without provocation.

CHAPTER NINETEEN

The secret of happiness is freedom.
The secret of freedom is courage.
— Thucydides

The darkness of the courtroom blocked out the brightness of the sun. The beautiful fall day included a gentle wind and the smell of leaves. Because autumn is my favorite season, I so want to be outside to enjoy the weather before the chill of winter sets in.

Nita sat right beside me for support. She attended the trial whenever her physical therapy job allowed. I found it comforting to feel Nita's presence while Ursula sat next to her. I smiled, knowing no one but I could see her. Most of my brothers and sisters sat in the benches behind me, except for Judith, who was still in the psychiatric ward. I could tell from their whispers that they were nervous. When I turned to look at them, Emma sent me the warmest smile she could manage.

"All rise," announced the deputy when Judge Christopher Buckman entered the courtroom. The air was thick with anticipation. The jury displayed no emotions, and it was hard for me to even think about what they had decided to do with my father.

"Has the jury reached a decision?" Judge Buckman asked. A woman rose and said the jury reached a decision. But before the judge asked her to read the verdict, he looked over at my father. "Reverend Thomas, will you please stand." It was a request and not a question.

My father slowly stood up. He had shaved that morning and his clothes were pressed. His eyes focused on the floor, and I could see his hands were shaking.

"Reverend Thomas, before the verdict is read, I'd like to hear if you have anything to say to the jury."

"Yes, your Honor. I'd like to say a few words." He turned and looked at the jury. "If you say I did what you claim, I'm sorry, but I don't remember a lot of the terrible acts that people said I did." He sat back down in his chair.

No one breathed in the courtroom. A sorrowful silence hung in the air for several minutes.

I was stunned by his total lack of responsibility. I lowered my head and could feel the anger burn in my heart and the bile forcing its way up my throat. I swallowed and shook my head. I closed my eyes to keep the tears from falling. "How could he deny what he did?" I asked myself.

"Has the jury reached a decision?" Judge Buckman asked.

The jury spokesperson handed a piece of paper to the deputy, who then brought it to the judge. Judge Buckman read the paper, folded it, and returned it to the deputy. The deputy handed the paper to the standing spokesperson.

She opened the paper. "The jury has found Reverend Thomas guilty as charged."

The judge nodded at the jury, then said, "In four weeks, I will sentence Reverend Thomas. He will continue to remain in custody without parole. Case closed." He banged his gavel and left the room.

There was no applause or cheers from the crowd. Most people quietly walked out of the courtroom with their heads down and their hands in their pockets. Clarence Southerly turned and whispered something into my father's ear. He then rose, shook his head, and put his notes in his briefcase.

Nita enfolded her arms around me and held me.

What was done was done, and it was now time for the law to take over. The waiting would soon be over.

CHAPTER TWENTY

Healing doesn't mean the damage never existed.
It means the damage no longer controls our lives.
— Unknown

When I finally felt I could emotionally trust my feelings, I decided to attempt a comeback, which was more difficult than I thought. This Saturday morning, Nita had to work at the hospital, and I had a day to myself, but I did not want to spend it alone. For some unknown reason, I suddenly needed to talk with Emma. I did not know the reason.

I rang the bell to her condo. Em opened the door and ushered me in. She was in disarray looking like she did not sleep all night.

"Em, are you okay?"

"Yeah, but I've been doing some research."

"Is this work-related?"

"No, it's family-related." Em pointed at a chair in her kitchen and made a fresh pot of coffee.

"What's up?"

"Adam and Ben came over last night to talk with me."

"This doesn't sound good."

"It isn't."

"What's going on with them?"

Em poured me a cup of coffee.

"They are really angry at Dad and themselves for not stopping the abuse."

"I wondered how long it would take for the truth to take root. So, what did they say?"

"They both knew Dad was hurting you and Mom, but they didn't do anything to stop it."

"Sounds like heavy-duty denial to me."

"Exactly." Em took a sip of her coffee and winced. "They don't understand why they chose to remain silent. I told them that their behavior fits into the abuse formula. I told them they were abused, too."

"Oh, I bet that didn't go over very well."

"Actually, they both agreed."

"Wow, that's amazing."

"Your testimony at Dad's trial opened their eyes and they can no longer be silent. And with Judith cutting her wrist, this pushed them into anger, despair, and embarrassment."

"So they knew they should have stepped in."

"That's where their shame comes in. Adam was disgusted with himself for letting the abuse continue for so many years. And, he's ashamed he blamed you for the problems in the family."

"They all betrayed me except for you."

"I told them that and it made them feel worse." Em reached out and held my hand. "Ben admitted that he's been thinking about suicide."

"What? Oh no!"

"I encouraged him to talk with a therapist in my clinic."

"Do you think he will?"

"I'm going to follow-up with him this afternoon. He needs to accept his part in this and he's scared."

"I know how that feels." I leaned back in my chair, pondering this news.

"Hey, you're the expert on betrayal. I encouraged both of them to seek counseling."

"I really hope they do. They're in for a long healing journey."
I paused, "Do they understand how much that betrayal hurt me?"

"They saw the results first-hand at the trial."

"But I forgive them."

"Amen to that Claud." Em used the nickname she called me since childhood. "They don't know how to apologize to you for their actions, or should I say nonactions."

"I told them that you forgive them, but they need to apologize to you and not me."

"I would welcome them back into my life with open arms."

"That's why I love you so much," Em smiled. "They both stated they're also concerned they will continue the abuse. Adam especially worries about his relationship with his wife and daughter."

Adam was married to Mia and their daughter Brooke was five years old.

"I imagine he's terrified that he'll abuse Mia and Brooke like Father did to Mom and you."

"That would be extremely scary since abuse cycles through one generation to the next."

"If not stopped."

I nodded. "Did they think they were in the clear believing the myth that abuse skips a generation?"

"Yeah, but they now know that's a very harmful public misconception."

"I'm sure it was. They must have been in shock when you told them the truth."

"They were horribly alarmed." Em poured us another cup of coffee. "That's why I'm going to call them both this afternoon, to see how they're coping with the information I gave them last night."

"Do they understand they need to accept their own responsibility, shame, and anger?"

"Oh, yeah. They just don't know where to start. That's why I gave them my co-therapist's contact info."

"I'm so happy we have a therapist in the family."

"I knew I had to pursue this line of work when I was in high school. I didn't know how to help you." Tears filled Em's eyes.

"Hey, you've always been there for me. I can never thank you enough for not abandoning me."

"I would never do that to you. I didn't know how to help you back then, but I was passionate about finding a way to support you."

"And I so appreciate your love and support, especially now, with helping Adam and Ben heal their own lives." I peered into my coffee cup. "Father almost destroyed our family. I'm relieved to know they don't want to follow in Father's footsteps. Do you think they'll ever confront Stan in prison?"

"I mentioned this, but they're too raw to face him."

"He'll always be a bully and a sociopathic narcissist."

"Absolutely." Em leaned toward me. "So when did you get your psychology degree?"

"Everything I know I learned from you." I snickered.

"Funny – not! I do, however, give you credit for your vast knowledge of child abuse from personal experience."

"You'd think I should have a Ph.D. by now." We both laughed, then I grew serious again. "You know I considered a career in psychology."

"Yes, but your passion is, and always has been, for writing."

I nodded. "Words are like puzzles to me because you have to understand the rules of writing before you can break a few."

"You break puzzles?"

"Boy are you on a roll this morning."

"It's all due to the amount of coffee I've had in the past twelve hours, but now back to our brothers."

"Right. So what can I do for Adam and Ben?"

"Be patient with them because they're not sure what to say to you, and afraid you hate them."

Tears seeped from my eyes. "Like I said, I don't hate them, and I never meant to hurt them with going public with our family secret."

"I believe they know that, but you have to give each of them time."

"You know I will."

"There's more."

"This doesn't sound good."

"Adam hit Mia in the face months before the trial. He was so angry with her for hating Dad. She knew something was terribly wrong with the family."

"Is she okay?"

"Yeah, but frightened by Adam's anger."

"Hmm, sounds like anger management is in his future."

"Of course. He was ashamed that he hit her. He hasn't hit her since."

"Thank you, Universe!"

"So true," Em got up and started pacing.

"Is there something else going on?" I was alarmed.

"I went to see Dad this past week in prison. I had to confront him for my own healing."

"What did he say?"

"He feels you tried to ambush him, and he still believes you were the cause of the problems. But, I can see in his eyes that he knows that isn't true. It's a new beginning for him."

"Yay, but he's in a hostile environment where anger and revenge are acceptable. One of the other inmates beat him up pretty bad. Prisoners don't particularly like child abusers."

"I've heard that," my mind was spinning with negative images. "I hope he's okay."

"He spent some time in the infirmary, but he's now back in his cell."

"Do you think that's justice?"

"No, but he's the reason he's in prison."

I rose from my chair and walked over to Em. "I'm glad to know you're taking care of yourself and your healing. Em, I love you."

"And I love you."

CHAPTER TWENTY-ONE

The emotion that can break your heart is sometimes the very one that heals it...
—Nicholas Sparks, At First Sight

At midnight, the stars lit up the sky. A sliver of the moon shone enough light, so I could see beyond the campfire. The cool late autumn night was the perfect type of weather I love to camp in. I sat alone at the campfire while Nita slept in our camper.

I found it hard to believe that I was back in my favorite campsite at Banning State Park. Here I was, dressed snugly in my black and red fleece and flannel jacket, a knit hat on my head, and leather gloves to keep my hands warm. My cup of chamomile tea had grown cold and sat neglected on a small cooler next to my lawn chair. I watched the hot flames in the campfire flicker in the night, and I recalled many of the dreams I had in front of past fires. I dreamed the abuse would end, and I would no longer be abused. I dreamed about being free of my father. I dreamed of owning my own place and having my own life. I dreamed of finding love.

A log cracked, and a spark flew out of the fire. I blinked as it dawned on me that all those dreams had come true. I was no longer the pitiful little girl I thought I was. I had grown into a woman who stood up for what was wrong. I revealed the family secret, I admitted that I was abused and tortured, and the people on the jury believed me. I wished them all my immeasurable thanks.

"Well, I'll be damned," I said to the night. "All my dreams have come true." I sat in the firelight listening to the night sounds and the gentle wind that stirred the fallen leaves on the ground. A perfect night for reflection and meditation and my moment to finally find peace.

The weeks since my father's sentencing raced by, but would never be forgotten. I still could remember Judge Buckman's words:

"Reverend Thomas, you have committed the most egregious case of child abuse I have ever witnessed in this courtroom. The statute of limitations does not apply in this case and I, hereby, sentence you to 35 years in prison without parole." He tapped his gavel, stood, and left the courtroom.

At the age of 70, I knew my father's sentence was a death sentence. He would never be free again. The pain was drained, and I knew in my heart that I had to find peace with myself for a past I could not change.

I peered into the campfire for advice as I had on so many other occasions. The yellow and orange color in the flames reminded me of long, fiery fingertips caressing the logs. The black holes in the logs reminded me of my scars, which were now faded, and though I knew the marks would remain, as would the memories, my heart informed me it was time to completely heal my emotional wounds.

I hated myself back then, feeling somehow responsible for what my father did, but that shame and guilt was now replaced with a self-love I had never known. The judge and the jury knew I told the truth and they took appropriate action. It amazed me that people actually believed me after all the years of being told by my father that I was a liar. I was not a liar. I shivered in the night, not from the cold, but from the knowledge that I told the truth. A warm feeling of love embraced me, and I hugged myself. It felt so good to live again and to feel love.

Nita was asleep in the camper, but her presence in my life, and the support she gave me during the trial, was mind-boggling. She loved me for being me. The first several weeks of our relationship were not easy for her. I had so much garbage to work through, but the weeks raced by as I began to understand the depth of love for myself and her. Her beautiful smile made my heart soar.

Nita opened my soul, and I noticed myself woozy with joy. Having never experienced this feeling before, I found myself intrigued by the intensity of carefree loving. Pain and suffering were nonexistent as the days flew. So many moments of delight made me feel both ecstatic and fearful that it might end. This was a new fear that I did not mind. Every morning, I am kissed with love, and every evening, I fall asleep knowing I am safe in the arms of an angel. I am truly blessed.

When I thought about my brothers, and all that Emma told me, I found their struggles overwhelming. Though I got through mine I wasn't unscathed, and my brothers wouldn't be either. Adam and Ben were now in therapy and Em was seeing progress. They now understand that child abuse is a poison and are wanting to eradicate it in their lives. I smiled as I remembered when they came to my apartment to apologize. They acted like two little boys who got stealing candy from the grocery store. I had to hide my smile as they asked for my forgiveness. I agreed to help them where I could and answer any questions. When it came time for them to leave, I gave them each a warm hug. I was so delighted when they hugged me back.

Staring into the flames again, I promised myself that I would do all I possibly could to support them and to make my relationship with Nita a gift of love for her and for me.

"Wow," I whispered into the autumn air. "I'm pretty amazing!" I laughed at my own discovery. I leaned back in my lawn chair and gazed at the stars. Out here in the forest, they were bright, and I could see the Big Dipper. I closed my eyes.

I heard branches break in the woods near the campfire. The sound startled me as I found two eyes looking at me. I rose quickly and awkwardly stepped back into my lawn chair, loudly collapsing behind me. I could feel my heart racing, and I glanced behind me to see how far I was from the camper. I was twenty feet from the door, too far away to run. I held my breath.

The black bear strolled into the campsite sniffing the air. "Grrrrr."

I knew from Ursula that black bears were omnivores, eating plants, fruits, insects, and occasionally killing young deer, but this last fact did not squelch my nerves. Lying on my collapsed lawn chair, I knew I was toast. I froze.

I heard the black bear come closer. I held my breath.

"Girl, I see all that physical therapy you had didn't help your balance," the bear chuckled if bears could chuckle.

"Ursula?" I whispered, trying to get up. Relief rushed through my veins.

"Didn't mean to startle you," Ursula said as she sat on her back legs. Her fur had the familiar uniform color with a black snout and white markings on her chest.

"Shit, I almost peed in my pants," I said, righting the lawn chair. I sat down but was still shaking.

"Well, well, same potty mouth I remember." Ursula shook her head. "I guess some things never change."

"I'm surprised to see you," I said, trying to calm my nerves.

"I was in the neighborhood and saw your campfire. Thought I'd say hello."

Though I knew it was really Ursula and not some attack animal, I carefully made my way to her. As I hugged her, I smelled a fresh pine scent on her fur, touched the softness, and leaned into her mass.

"I see that you've been staring into the campfire like so many times before."

"You've been here before?"

"Yes, but you were so afraid back then. Every dark shadow spooked you, and every time I walked close to your campsite, you'd run into your pop-up camper, and crawl under your blankets. I was so surprised you came back by yourself."

"I love this place, and I came here to heal."

"And you have. What did the fire tell you tonight?"

I thought about Ursula's question for several minutes. I was not sure I knew the answer. "I learned that I was never responsible for what Stan did, and I'm not responsible for the punishment he received. The judge and jury were very wise, and they saw how much he hurt me."

"A number of jurors shed tears as they left the courtroom at the end."

"Really, Ursula?"

"Really."

I could feel my own tears stinging my eyes, or was it from the campfire smoke?

"Claudia, look at me."

When I did, I started to sob. I could not stop myself. The tears ran down my face like a waterfall, and I could do nothing but let them go. I finally found my voice.

"I stopped my father, but I can't stop all parents who abuse their children."

"Claudia, your ancestors want to say something to you about this."

"They do? Are they here?" I looked around the silent campsite.

On the other side of the fire pit, I saw an Indian Chief walk out of the woods with several women behind him. He was dressed in a long rectangular piece of tanned deerskin called a breechcloth. He wore the cloth in between his legs and tucked over a belt. His dark-skinned shoulders and chest were hidden behind a beaded breastplate. A roach headdress made of colored deer fur and porcupine framed his head. He was so impressive looking. He nodded at me as I stood.

"I am Chief White Wolf. I am here tonight to bless your presence and guide your future. Your ancestors are here with me. They want to say a few words to you so you understand what they ask of you." He raised both of his hands to the night sky.

A woman about five feet tall appeared dressed in a dull-colored petticoat made from cheap and coarse material, a worn jacket to match, a pair of black stockings, and a white mop hat. Her skin was very dry, and her facial features were aged and expressionless.

"I am Claudia Mary Matthews, your great, great, great aunt. My children and I were beaten by my husband until I poisoned his drink with arsenic. When he died, I was arrested and imprisoned for his murder. I spent the rest of my life in prison until I died." She bowed and backed up to disappear into the dark.

Another woman emerged wearing an ashen-colored straight, curve-less dress. Her waist was completely hidden and the belt she wore was around her hips. I immediately thought her apparel looked like that of the 1920s.

"I am your great, great paternal grandmother Rose Thomas. My husband stabbed and killed me with a knife as I was defending our three children from his brutal beatings." She, too, stepped back into the darkness.

Chief White Wolf lowered his hands. His deep voice shuddered, "There is someone else who wants to speak with you."

Another woman emerged from the dark, but this time I knew who she was. Dressed in a long skirt and a long-sleeved blouse, I recognized my mother.

"My dear Claudia. I'm so sorry for all the pain and suffering you've experienced. I was responsible for your safety, but I did not have the courage to do what you've done. Like many of your ancestors, it is the women who took the brutality of our children to our graves, never stopping the violent men who bestowed so much terror on our children. Together, we ask for your forgiveness for failing our children. We're proud of what you've done, and the justice you uncovered in this lifetime. We cannot forget the past, but your ancestors and I know you are the new beginning to a world without child and domestic abuse. You have the strength and fortitude to turn your generation into a non-violent world, one that can stop the abuse of children and women. I ask you to remember the men who have been abused for they are often the forgotten ones. They too, have suffered and need to be healed. Please, Claudia, forgive all your ancestors and me for what we couldn't do to stop this epidemic of abuse."

I watched my mother feeling as though my heart would suddenly shatter. So many tears lined up wanting to spill down my cheeks, but I held them back for fear I would never stop crying.

These beautiful women, my ancestors, had tried to right the wrongs of their husbands but were imprisoned or killed. They, too, needed justice and the promise that I would try to end child and domestic abuse.

"Mom, and all my beloved ancestors, I will do as you ask to the very best of my abilities. Please know that I forgive you all and love you all so much. I need your combined strength to help me in this fight. I will never forget you."

With that, I saw Chief White Wolf bow and walk out of the light of the campfire along with my ancestors.

I shook my head. Did I really see what I did? Was I dreaming?

"Claudia, no one has the right to do to children what your father did to you. No one." Ursula shifted on her back legs. "The damage your father did no longer controls you. You are truly free."

I could only nod at her words.

"You did what you needed to do to empower yourself. So many abused children continue to take it until they die. You didn't. Your gift to these children is to show them how to survive."

I nodded.

Ursula's voice traveled calmly over the firelight. "Your ancestors are so proud of you."

"I didn't think I could stay sane through the trial, the memories, or face my brothers and sisters," I solemnly stated.

"But you did and look what happened, people believed you. Now you need to tell your story, so others can survive."

"Sounds like a mission," I said with a smile.

"And a purpose," Ursula added.

I yawned suddenly and glanced at my watch. It was two o'clock in the morning.

"Feeling content?"

"Very," I answered. "And sleepy."

"Then I suggest that we end this delightful evening. There's a special woman in your life who loves and adores you, and needs you now." Ursula pointed to the camper with her large paw.

Her words made me smile. "Yeah, you're right."

"Empower others, Claudia, and bring an end to this ugly war on humanity. Child abuse stops with you, remember that." She paused. "Now, I suggest you proceed into that camper and wrap yourself in all that love."

"I will," I smiled again and started walking to the camper. At the door I stopped, turned, and watched Ursula wander out of the campsite and into the dark forest.

"Thank you, Ursula, my divine guardian bear."

EPILOGUE

A Note from Claudia

Dear Reader,

Child abuse has been going on for centuries and needs to be stopped for all the suffering it brings to children and families. In 2010, the Catholic Church was publicly criticized and condemned for its ill-treatment and abuse of children and nuns by priests. In 2017, hundreds of women marched together to call out sexual harassment in the workplace. Now it is time to sound the alarm in our homes and report the sexual, emotional, psychological, and spiritual damage done to children and women.

Child and domestic abuse are unethical and wrong, and the cycle of abuse must be stopped forever.

Tell your story. If you see or know of a child in danger, report it to the authorities and save that child's life.

Be a guardian bear!

THE END

ABOUT THE AUTHOR

Alexis Acker-Halbur

Award winning author, Alexis Acker-Halbur, has published four books and four e-books, and over a dozen magazine articles and three poems published in literary magazines. Her book, *Never Give Up: Break the Connection Between Stress and Illness*, won the 2018 Living Now Evergreen Gold Medal Book Award. This award is given to books that change people's lives.

Alexis is a professional trauma expert helping survivors recover from dramatic personal experiences to live a healthy and purposeful life. You can follow her on her website: **https://nevergiveupinstitute.org.**

RESOURCES

NATIONAL RESOURCES FOR VICTIMS AND
SURVIVORS OF DOMESTIC VIOLENCE &
NATIONAL CRISIS ORGANIZATIONS AND
ASSISTANCE:

The National Domestic Violence Hotline
1-800-799-7233 (SAFE)
www.ndvh.org

National Dating Abuse Helpline
1-866-331-9474
www.loveisrespect.org

National Child Abuse Hotline/Childhelp
1-800-4-A-CHILD (1-800-422-4453)
www.childhelp.org
www.childhelpusa.org

National Sexual Assault Hotline
1-800-656-4673 (HOPE)
www.rainn.org

National Suicide Prevention Lifeline
1-800-273-8255 (TALK)
www.suicidepreventionlifeline.org

National Resource Center on Domestic Violence
1-800-537-2238
www.nrcdv.org and www.vawnet.org

**Futures Without Violence: The National Health Resource
Center on Domestic Violence**
1-888-792-2873
www.futureswithoutviolence.org

National Center on Domestic Violence, Trauma & Mental Health
1-312-726-7020 ext. 2011
www.nationalcenterdvtraumamh.org

Domestic Violence Initiative
(303) 839-5510/ (877) 839-5510
www.dviforwomen.org

Deaf Abused Women's Network (DAWN)
Email: Hotline@deafdawn.org
VP: 202-559-5366
www.deafdawn.org

INCITE! Women of Color Against Violence
incite.natl@gmail.com
www.incite-national.org

Casa de Esperanza
Linea de crisis 24-horas/24-hour crisis line
1-651-772-1611
www.casadeesperanza.org

National Indigenous Women's Resource Center
855-649-7299
www.niwrc.org

Asian and Pacific Islander Institute on Domestic Violence
1-415-954-9988
www.apiidv.org

Institute on Domestic Violence in the African American Community
1-877-643-8222
www.dvinstitute.org

The Black Church and Domestic Violence Institute
1-770-909-0715
www.bcdvi.org

The Audre Lorde Project
1-178-596-0342
www.alp.org

LAMBDA GLBT Community Services
1-206-350-4283
http://www.qrd.org/qrd/www/orgs/avproject/main.htm

Northwest Network of Bisexual, Trans, Lesbian & Gay Survivors of Abuse
1-206-568-7777
www.nwnetwork.org

National Clearinghouse on Abuse in Later Life
1-608-255-0539
www.ncall.us

National Center for Elder Abuse
1-855-500-3537
www.aginginplace.org

Men Stopping Violence
1-866-717-9317
www.menstoppingviolence.org

Legal Momentum
1-212-925-6635
www.legalmomentum.org

Womenslaw.org
www.womenslaw.org

National Clearinghouse for the Defense of Battered Women
1-800-903-0111 x 3
www.ncdbw.org

[Source: https://ncadv.org/resources]

In Minnesota, please contact:

Sexual Violence Center (Minneapolis, MN)
https://www.sexualviolencecenter.org/

MN Trauma Therapist Directory
https://www.mntraumaproject.org/mn-trauma-therapist-directory

Trauma and PTSD Therapists in Minnesota
https://www.psychologytoday.com/us/therapists/trauma-andptsd/minnesota

NAMI – National Alliance on Mental Illness
http://www.namihelps.org/

The Minnesota Warmline
https://mentalhealthmn.org/support/minnesota-warmline/

Mental Health MN
https://mentalhealthmn.org/about/about-us/